Dear Cathy,
Thanks so much
taking part in
Hope you enjoy
   Best wishes,
      Amanda

THE WORD

FOR

FREEDOM

Edited by
Amanda Saint
and
Rose McGinty

Retreat West Books
https://retreatwestbooks.com

For everyone, everywhere,
who believes in freedom and equality for all

CONTENTS

FOREWORD

This anthology celebrates a hundred years of women's suffrage, with stories inspired by the suffragettes and also stories from today about many of the same freedoms that those women fought for so courageously.

When the suffragettes were marching on Westminster under the banner of 'Deeds Not Words', women writers of the time were also taking up their pens in solidarity. The authors Cicely Hamilton and Bessie Hatton formed the Women Writers' Suffrage League in 1908. The League gained over four hundred members, women and men, and its aim was 'to obtain the Parliamentary Franchise for women on the same terms as it is, or may be, granted to men. Its methods are the methods proper to writers – the use of the pen.' The women writers knew that words were as important as deeds as they could tell the stories to bring about social reform and freedom from patriarchal oppression.

Delving into the personal histories of the women writers in the League, such as Elizabeth Robins, Beatrice Harraden, Ivy Compton-Burnett and Sarah Grand, and the subjects they wrote about, chimed immediately with the themes explored in this anthology: equality, freedom, power struggles, harrassment, the right to an education, health matters, sexuality, parenthood, employment rights, marriage and war. Women may have won the vote and equality legislation has secured the rights of many people who face discrimination, but we are still fighting the same battles today. We still need words for freedom.

The idea for this collection came when I heard about the One Hundred Year March, which would be following in the footsteps of the Bow suffragettes as they marched to the Houses of Parliament. The organisers wanted to hold the march to give a voice to women from communities in the East End who are often not heard, continue to shine a light on social issues and raise money for charities like Hestia, which supports people in crisis. They were keen for artists, musicians, writers and creatives to be inspired by the march and develop projects in its spirit. At the time I was working for the NHS in the East End and conscious as I walked the same streets as the suffragettes of the need to celebrate their stories, and seeing the deprivation and suffering still deeply rooted in society to give a voice to today's issues. I approached Amanda Saint of Retreat West Books because I knew that she has a deep commitment to finding new writing voices and supporting social causes. Without a second's hesitation Amanda said yes and very quickly we were joined by a number of passionate women writers who offered to donate stories. We opened a competition to find new voices too and the result is this beautiful, thought provoking anthology. Jennie Rawlings wrapped it all together with her stunning cover design and we are honoured that Marian Keyes, Laline Paull and Isabel Ashdown agreed to give their generous words of support.

Through this anthology we are proud to support Hestia and the UK Says No More campaign against domestic abuse and sexual violence, www.uksaysnomore. org. Hestia works with over 9,000 adults and children experiencing domestic abuse, modern slavery, mental health needs and in crisis across London every year, find out more at www.hestia.org.

Back in 1918 members of the Women Writers' Suffrage League used their plays, novels, and writing to increase awareness of a wide range of women's issues. They recognised that there was nothing more powerful than a story to draw the hearts and minds of people across the country to their cause. We hope that a hundred years later, with this collection, which echoes so many of the original and enduring causes of the suffragettes, the stories here will capture reader's hearts and minds and inspire them to become involved with charities, such as Hestia, and campaigns like the UK Says No More. In this way words may become deeds.

Thank you to everyone who has supported this anthology.

Rose McGinty

The Word For Freedom

Isabel Costello

WHEN MY CHILDREN sprang this trip on me, it was an unwanted gift. They had to remind me: *Mum, it's something you've always wanted to do.* As the only solo traveller I sat wherever there was space, never with the same people twice; quiet and invisible, as always. As we bumped along the rutted track, Nkomo and Justin spoke to each other in a curious mix of English, Afrikaans and a language I later discovered was Shangaan. I loved the animal stories Justin told us. A spotted hyena can tell another's age, sex and status by a single note of their call. I thought about whether people could match that – a sentence, a word, yes; but a single syllable?

Justin kept reaching for the radio to share news of our sightings with other vehicles, sometimes receiving the signal for a new chase to begin. Now the sun was up, everyone was over the miserable five o'clock wake-up call. As the radio crackled into life on the dashboard once more, I recognised the word *ingwe*, the Zulu name for leopard. Replacing the handset, Justin grinned at Nkomo in the jumpseat up front, the two of them like schoolboys in their game lodge caps. It wasn't another leopard, he told us, it was better. He threw the jeep into reverse, planting the heel of his hand at the base of the steering wheel and spinning it round. 'If anyone asks, we didn't go this fast,' he said, the exhilaration in his voice infectious. The jeep had no sides so falling out was a real possibility. With another jolt, it left the track and tore across the bush, driving straight over small trees which popped up like they were on springs. It made me look back every time, made me want to laugh. Something else I'd forgotten.

'Watch out on the left!' shouted Justin, too late. The thorn bush tore at my face but nobody heard my cries. I pulled my floppy hat down and tried to breathe through the stinging. Behind my sunglasses, my eyes were watering.

The Zulu word for cheetah is *ingululu*.

We sat for a long time watching a female crunch through the skin, flesh and bone of a baby impala with the ease of eating rare steak. I looked away when she started on a gelatinous mass of entrails, rising from her haunches every few minutes to check for predators, looking straight at us with total indifference. Her head seemed too small for such a lithe magnificent body and when someone asked *why the collar?* Justin told us she'd escaped from a game farm hundreds of miles away in another part of the Kruger. Now she was free. Her face made me forget about mine. It's cheetahs, not leopards, who have spots.

I had scratches – lots of them. I brought my hand towards my burning cheek and could sense the tender stripes without touching the skin. When we met up with another group for coffee, the tanned blonde woman who'd been sitting in front of me looked up as she tore open a sachet of Nescafé.

'Oh my God!' she said. 'What's happened to you?'

Justin was over in an instant followed by Nkomo, who covered his mouth. I wanted to tell him my face didn't matter that much to me. His young skin was flawlessly smooth, so dark it almost had a purple in it.

'It's my fault,' I said, interrupting their apologies. 'You told us to duck.'

The woman helped me back onto the jeep, gave me coffee and got in beside me. Justin rifled through a First Aid kit for a tube of antiseptic cream.

'We'll head straight back to clean it up properly,' he said.

'Do you want me to do it?' asked the woman. 'I used to be a nurse.'

She'd had something done to her face. I couldn't work it out, but her eyes – the part that can't be changed – reflected light from the diamond studs in her ears. Even at this hour, she was wearing mascara.

'My name's Hilary,' she said. 'But everyone calls me Hill.'

'As in *Over the hill!*' came a brash voice from the group of men eating muffins. I could guess who it was: the only one laughing. Hill's face didn't move, except for one corner of her mouth, very slightly.

'Don't mind him. That's my husband, Peter.'

In the early months without George, I put a note next to the kettle reminding me to make only one hot drink. I didn't want my family to worry, so it didn't say HE'S GONE or WIDOW. It said BUY TEABAGS.

They must have thought I drank a lot of tea.

Back at the lodge, the manager called a doctor from the nearest town. 'There's still a thorn in there,' he said. 'Best see to it quickly with this big storm coming.' We'd seen dark clouds rolling across from the Blyde River Canyon as we drove back.

I refused the anaesthetic spray; I'd had enough of numbness. I could feel the doctor digging around with fine tweezers trying to extract the broken thorn.

I could *feel*.

'There,' he showed me the vicious spike before taping a small dressing over the wound. 'You'll be back to normal in no time.'

He couldn't have known that was the last thing I wanted.

4

The days were odd, starting too early and lasting too long with a constant sense of waiting for the next meal or game drive. Back in my chalet, sleep wouldn't come and the balcony with its flimsy woven roof was no place to sit and read in a storm. The sky was darkening by the second; the temperature had dropped a good ten degrees and the sounds of the bush faded almost to silence in deference to the wind. So I lay flat on the pristine covers of the enormous bed. In the absence of the usual heat, the polished steel fan hung motionless above me, the large disc in the centre acting as a mirror which the rotating blades had previously prevented me from noticing.

I looked so small against that expanse of white. Although I couldn't see myself distinctly, or maybe because of that, something made me think of myself as a young woman. I was a teacher when I first met my husband. My name wasn't *Mum* or *Grandma*. It wasn't *Dear* either. I always wished he wouldn't call me that. I had lost all notion of myself except in relation to people who didn't need me anymore. Instead of a class of children, I'd had a houseful. Five, all but one married now, with families of their own.

Like shouting, you get used to the sound of thunder. It was different in South Africa, not cracking but detonating and booming, a series of explosions. When it moved directly overhead I looked up and saw myself in the metal reflection of the fan: tense with fear, yet awash with relief at being alone.

I thought of the cheetah, still wearing a collar even though she was free.

As the storm began to retreat, I opened the door and listened to the rain changing in volume and intensity, as though it had different settings, and I was overcome with the beauty of it all.

'Hello there,' said a voice, disconcertingly near. 'It's only me, Hill. How are you doing?'

My left cheek was still throbbing.

With less chance of spotting game after a storm, there weren't many takers for the afternoon drive. 'You'll still come, eh?' asked Hill, as if it mattered to her.

It was the whole reason I was there, and I didn't want Justin and Nkomo to feel bad about what had happened. Hill's husband Peter ignored me when she tried to introduce us and sat pointedly alone in the middle row of seats. We sat behind.

'He's more of a man's man,' she said quietly. 'He works in mining, you know. It's a hard life.'

The bit I *knew* about was being married to a man like him, and constantly having to smooth everything over: with the children, with relatives and neighbours. I dismissed Peter's rudeness with a smile and fell back on the conversation I kept hearing all around me. 'Have you been on safari before?'

'*Ja*, many times,' said Hill. 'We're marking our 25th

wedding anniversary.'

An odd way to put it, not *We're celebrating*. But maybe they weren't. Maybe they *were* just marking time. George and I had a 25ᵗʰ anniversary and were only a couple of years off our 40th. To the very end he wanted the last word, when he clutched at his chest and his eyes rolled off to the side. On reflection, a single human syllable can convey quite a lot.

It wouldn't help Hill if I told her George died a year ago, to the day.

We came across a pack of lions. Two enormous males roared and paced astonishingly close to us. Justin whispered to stay completely still. Eventually they lost interest and returned to the pride, stretching and grooming themselves like pet cats.

'I've dropped it,' Peter said loudly.

'Sssh,' hissed Justin. 'If you drop a lens cap here, you won't see it again.'

'I mean the whole bloody camera,' said Peter. 'We need to get it back.'

It lay there in the dust, long lens pointing up in the air.

'You *can't*,' said Justin, 'and that's the end of it.'

Peter's huge back inflated and his shoulders rose at least six inches. Beside me, I heard Hill gulp. 'Listen to him, *liefling*.'

Peter shook himself free of her hand. 'That's a 10,000

rand camera. *He* should fetch it,' he said, jerking his head at Nkomo. 'He's practically one of them.'

We all gaped at him in horror. An earnest young man whose first language wasn't English dared to say, 'You are asking a man to risk his life.'

Except that he wasn't *asking*.

From the jumpseat Nkomo looked at Peter, unmoved. As the tracker, he didn't often speak to guests. 'I will not do it.'

Then Peter stood up, which was not allowed. 'You people! You're all the fucking same. I'll get it myself.'

'Sit down please, sir,' said Justin. 'The second you step off the vehicle the lions will see you as prey.'

But Peter jumped, falling forwards onto his hands. I had a vision of Justin starting the engine and leaving him to be devoured. Beside me, Hill covered her eyes. One of the male lions glanced over his shoulder just as Peter heaved himself back onto the jeep, brandishing the camera in triumph.

I couldn't bear to think of Hill having to listen to this story for the rest of their lives.

'Right, that's it, I'm calling it a day,' said Justin, shaking his head as we slowly reversed away.

Peter turned to his wife but she got in first. 'Don't you even look at me, Peter. I will never forgive you for this.'

There would be no sundowners today. Halfway back

to the lodge, Hill and I exchanged a look. I was the first to reach for the ring on my finger. In a synchronised motion, we hurled them into the next thorn bush we passed. '*Vryheid*,' she said, with a smile.

Counting For England

Christine Powell

IF HE WERE to make an inventory of his life and then to pick a moment that initiated and defined his current disquiet, the night of April 2nd 1911 would appear underscored three times in the records.

Initially, what really irked him was the lack of respect for an occasion that represented the summit of human achievement. His mother had taught him to count things as soon as he was able: how many forks in a drawer? How many loaves on the kitchen table? How many wooden pegs in the clothes basket? Bullfinches in the plum trees? Pellets in a gun?

And how many bricks to build a barn, stones to construct a wall, grains of sand in the mortar to bind them? How many hairs on his daughter's head? How many hairs in a horse's mane, betting slips locked in his desk, touts on the Downs on Derby Day?

Percy Edgar Ridge, clerk of works at the Palace of Westminster, could count for England. So, the National

Census, all subjects named, numbered, placed and accounted for was, for him, a thing of joy. At 10.30 p.m., he collected the form for the House of Commons permanent household and began his rounds.

The debates had finished early to allow the members to travel to their residences; the bars were closed, he'd checked the benches for dozing or drunken parliamentarians, and now the dark corridors, their reek of damp, brandy and cigar smoke, the swaggering echoes of the day's work, were his as he walked from the Strangers' Gallery to the Undercroft, from crown to crypt, closing up, shutting down.

In the Undercroft, he counted fourteen paces from the bottom of the steps to the door of St. Mary's Chapel. A few points of candle-light still burned near the altar; he collected the snuffer from its hook next to the broom cupboard in the south west corner and had just turned back towards the eastern end when he heard something. Too insistent for rats, too loud for drips of condensation; firm, regular raps coming from inside the cupboard. Percy was a sober, country-bred rationalist. He was not nervous or highly strung. He did not believe in ghosts.

'Is somebody out there?'

Percy Edgar Ridge placed his hand flat on the cool stone architrave around the door to steady himself. Working in the House of Commons had largely inured him to bizarre behaviour, but this was outrageous! There was a woman in his broom cupboard.

'Would you like to explain why you are hiding in there, Miss?'

Of course, he should have hauled her out forthwith – but she had blockaded the door. He should have called the police straightaway, but he thought he could handle her. To engage in conversation, to let her think, therefore, he might be persuaded, *that* was the fatal mistake.

Because she told him why. And she had an answer for everything. She wanted her name recorded on his form. She asked him if he had a daughter, as if she knew that was the way to soften him up. One thing he knew: he would never want Connie to stick her neck out, to put herself in danger the way this woman and her associates did.

'Am I in danger now?' she said.

He had to admit that no, she was in no immediate danger. 'But you must be very uncomfortable, Miss.'

She had a seat on an upturned bucket and room to stretch her limbs among the brooms and mops, that was luxury, she said, compared to being in a cell in Holloway Prison. And as she talked, he realised who was talking. This woman's reputation went before her and now he feared for his broom cupboard, for his little chapel, for his whole world. What might she have in there with her? Tins of red paint? Rags and fire-lighters?

So, they made a deal. He would write her name on

the form, it would be officially recorded. She would be counted as a resident of the House of Commons. He couldn't grasp the point, see how this small gesture would change anything, but he would do it. Then he'd call the police. Which was what she expected.

'So, Percy,' she said, as she emerged from the cupboard, 'a woman can now lay claim to the same political rights as men.'

He smiled at this absurdity, and perhaps everything would still have been all right if only …. But she kept him talking, about how Mrs. Ridge would have no truck with suffragettes; about the life he wanted for his little girl; about justice and equality (even though he deferred to her as Miss Davison and she addressed him as Percy) and how they both loved horses. Epsom Downs on Derby Day, the thrill of the big race … and then he said, 'now that would be quite something, Miss, to stop the King's horse!'

It was just words! He wasn't serious. But she was. 'Deeds, not words,' was her credo and the idea took root until it haunted her as it haunts him now. So when the sadness overwhelms him, he goes down to the broom cupboard and sits on an upturned bucket for a while, to remember. Emily, he can call her Emily now she is dead, was a fierce, awkward, obstreperous woman. And, for a few hours, they were friends.

Below The Line

Victoria Richards

THE FIRST COMMENT comes with a self-righteous whiff of semen. 'Who is this "woman"?', in intermittent and indignant Caps Lock. 'Who IS she?'

I sit beneath the window, bottle of beer in hand, pondering my enforced existential crisis. It is almost nine in the evening. I left work hours ago. I only turned my laptop on out of an egotistical desire to see how many 'shares' I'd had. And I knew, of course I knew what I would find when I got there. You don't write a column about sexism without attracting the attention of pigs.

My index finger caresses the circular wheel of the mouse like a clit, scrolling, scrolling. ninety-six comments. I raise an eyebrow, take a swig of warm lager. I know I shouldn't, but I can't help myself. And I'm amused, at least at first. *Who AM I?* I've wondered that myself, half cut on a bottle of wine, gazing out at the street with the lights off. I like to watch them out there, courting, weaving, fighting, fucking. A voyeur to savagery.

'Silly slut,' they froth as I read on, sounding strangely Victorian. 'Whore,' they self-congratulate. 'Stupid bitch,' they spit. And then they get personal. 'I would,' one says, like he's being complimentary. 'You blind?' another counters. 'You'd have to wear beer goggles to fuck *that*.'

I imagine them sitting at home in identikit fury behind the smooth, safe glass of their computer monitors, keyboard warriors, anti-heroes, trolls. They are united in their desire to slash me, inch by column inch, dissect my margins, decapitate my byline.

'Ugly', they spew, 'evil', a 'sanctimonious hypocrite'. A 'self-serving, middle-class princess making a power grab by bullying women and demonising men,' part of an 'utterly loathsome creed.' I sit back, stung. Despite myself, despite everything, 'ugly' wounds me.

'She obviously can't get a bloke,' types Steve_365. 'Someone should rape her, teach her a lesson.' I shut down the screen without turning the power off.

Later that evening, my dad calls. 'I'm worried you're getting a reputation,' he says.

'As a bit of a… "feminist".' This, he whispers.

I roll my eyes, make platitudes. Before I go to bed I tap out a message to Steve_365. 'Thanks for the feedback,' I reply, evenly. 'Can we meet to discuss? I'm writing an article on trolling.'

I turn and bury my face into the coldness of the pillow. Perhaps I've only got myself to blame. Everyone says never read the comments.

A WEEK PASSES, then I'm sitting in a trendy café on a building site in Hackney, waiting for Steve_365. It is five in the afternoon and close to closing. The waitress has gone out the back to smoke a fag. I am jumpy, keep my hand on my phone. I'm ninety per cent sure Steve_365's rape threats were just that – threats – but you can't be too careful.

The door creaks and a pale, overweight man in his mid-thirties comes in. He's wearing a red football shirt. He doesn't meet my eyes.

'Steve?' I stand, think about putting my hand out to shake his, then retract it and wipe it on my jeans instead.

'It's Phil, actually,' he mumbles, staring at the dirty lino. He scrapes a chair along the floor and sits down warily, a metre or so from me. There's a brown stain beneath his collar. I sit back down.

'Thanks for coming,' I say. 'I think it's really brave, actually,' I add, fishing around in my bag.

'What is?' Steve, or Phil, pipes up. He lights a cigarette, despite the ban, leaving it to hang limply from the corner of his mouth, ash wrinkled to the tip like foreskin.

'You,' I say, bringing my hand to my lap. 'Agreeing to meet me like this. After the things you said.'

Phil's doughy cheeks redden. 'Look, that was just a joke, okay?'

I shrug. 'Okay.'

He looks uncertain.

'It doesn't matter,' I continue, 'you'll still be able to help me – with my article, I mean.'

I take out the knife and place it on the table between us. It lies there, gloriously erect, a full 12 inches of steel.

'As I said,' I continue, 'I'm writing about castration. I'm so glad you could contribute.'

Women Don't Kill Animals

Carolyn Sanderson

FAR ACROSS THE ocean, so they say, lies a great nation, where everyone is equal, everyone is free. When pressed or in their cups, they claim that once it was like that here; but that cannot be true. It's a comforting myth for those who have no hope in this life. Once, they say, you could reach it, reach this fabled place. Great boats crossed the waters, taking many days. I've heard it said that some of the boats could fly, but whoever could conceive of such a thing? Here, life is always hard. My mother says I think too much. Thinking does not gather firewood or sweep away the ashes of last night's fire. Thinking does not dig for the clay to make new cooking pots, or weave cloth for new tunics.

When I was a small child I was free to wander down to the shore and watch the men at their fishing. I liked to taste the salt on the breeze and listen to the swish of the waves as they hit the rocks. I would sit, my toes burrowing into the wet sand, watching and thinking about the stories I'd heard, of a time before the world became a different place and the great waters swelled.

Others were watching too, mostly boys. I sat apart from them. One day the tall one with the strangely coloured hair came over to where I was sitting.

'You're a girl,' he said.

I stared at him. It was something I knew and didn't know. Of course I knew that my body was made differently; having brothers had shown me that. Having sisters had shown me that there were things girls must do, and many that they must not. Girls would grow to be like their mothers, tending the home, bringing babies out of their bellies, offering the men the first of all the food they prepared, and going hungry if there wasn't enough.

What I didn't know was: why? Why did being a girl mean you didn't get to go fishing when you were big enough, or sit late at night around the fire drinking the beer the women made? Why was my father all-powerful in our home, while my mother cooked and cleaned and ensured we had warm clothes when the nights turned chilly, but was allowed no opinions of her own? It always seemed to me that we could have lived perfectly well without my father telling us what was permitted and what wasn't, but we wouldn't have survived a single day without our mother's care.

So when the strange boy accused me of being a girl that day, and I both knew and didn't know, it was

because I was too young to know why that made me
different. We both had arms and legs and feet to run
with, we both liked to dance and sing and listen to the
stories. If anyone was different, it was him, with his hair
the colour of polished copper whipping around his face in
the ocean breeze.

'So?' I said.

'So what are you doing here?'

'What are *you* doing?' I countered.

'Watching the men so I will know how to fish when I
am old enough.'

'That's what I'm doing too.'

He didn't reply to that. I could see his thoughts passing across his face. He was puzzled. Then one of the men
called,

'Lucas! What are you doing? Come and hold this rope
for me. This is no time to be talking to girl children.'

Lucas gave me a sort of lopsided grin, as though to say
sorry for something, and then he ran off to do as he was
told.

THAT WASN'T THE last I saw of Lucas. He was hard to
miss with that hair of his. The next time was at the Year's
Height Festival, when the whole village gathered to
celebrate the harvest. The grown-ups had eaten their fill,
and even the children had been handed enough scraps to

satisfy them. A great fire had been lit, right in the centre of the circle, and there was singing and dancing, the women at one side, the men at the other. I thought my father looked most undignified, but when I looked closely I could see that everyone's father looked like that. We children made our own music just outside the circle, with drums fashioned from animal skins which we stretched across the cooking pots we'd smuggled from the kitchen. Some of the older ones played on reed pipes, and there was laughter and singing and story-telling of the boastful kind small children indulge in.

'My father killed a wild boar last week.'

'*My* father killed two wild boars!'

'My father felled an oak tree *all by himself.* And he built a boat out of it.'

I decided to join in. 'My mother killed a wolf that was attacking the flock.'

There was general laughter.

'No she didn't!'

'Yes she did!'

'She couldn't have – not your *mother!*'

More laughter. I could feel the hot tears springing, and I looked around for help. Then he was there, the boy with hair that gleamed red in the firelight.

'Come with me.' He led and I followed, over to where the grown-ups had settled back in their seats. Ducking down, he crawled beneath one of the tables, and I piled in after him, a little clumsily. Above our heads mugs of beer were slammed onto the wooden boards, making us jump, and then the voices of people enjoying themselves became a background murmur.

'Why did you say that? About your mother?'

'It's true – she did.'

'No it's not.'

'Yes it is.'

He gave a sort of patient sigh, like my father does sometimes. He was older than me, and he was a boy. 'She couldn't have. Women don't kill animals.'

IT WAS ONLY later, after we had become friends, that I discovered who his father was. It was another festival, another time of hiding under tables. We had discovered that this was the way to hear things we weren't supposed to know.

'There is news from up north. The Headman has called a meeting.'

The speaker was one of the important men, a village elder. I recognised his voice, for he was often at our house giving my father a hard time. We were falling behind in our share. Then we heard a blast on the horns that meant something important was about to happen. Lucas and I put our fingers in our ears against the noise until it ceased and held our breath as we saw the village elder's feet planted firmly on the ground in front of us. There was a general shuffling as all the rest of the men got to their feet and the women, who were already on their feet serving the food, moved off as swiftly as they could towards the Women's House.

I had never seen the village Headman before, but even without his richly decorated cloak and staff of office, I would have guessed who he was, for he stood straight and tall and perfectly at ease in his own body. This was not a man who laboured in the fields. His hands, resting on the staff, showed pale, clean skin. My eyes travelled up from ground level where I lay, finally reaching his hair and beard. They were the colour of copper. Lucas groaned.

'Now I'm for it.'

'Your father?'

He nodded.

'Just keep still.'

The Headman spoke of messengers who had arrived, ahead of a great body of people in search of new lands. They claimed they came in peace, but according to our own spies, they came prepared for war. That made sense to me as I always tried to be prepared for any eventuality; so on cloudy days I still took a covering with me in case the sun's harmful rays should suddenly blaze through the clouds. It didn't mean that I knew for certain what the weather would do, but I was ready for whatever happened.

There was a great deal of discussion afterwards, which Lucas and I were too sleepy to follow, until eventually we heard the Headman say,

'I thank you, men of this land. We've heard many voices raised in favour of war, and some in favour of waiting to see what these strangers want. We'll meet again tomorrow for further debate. For now, let our festivities resume.' A cheer erupted at this pronouncement, and the women reappeared as if by magic, carrying jugs of beer and boards piled high with fruits and food of all kinds. The Storyteller rose to his feet, and there was more cheering and some stamping of feet. He was popular with everyone, but I had never really listened to his stories before. That night I did.

That is when I first learnt of the Great Catastrophe, the thing that had changed our whole world. This was in the time before, when women had been in charge and they had become greedy. They had wanted more and more, and the men had been forced to burn up the ancient buried forests to make the things the women demanded. The burning had changed the sky above our heads, had caused the great floodwaters to swell, but still the women refused to acknowledge the harm they were doing. They had formed armies, and squabbled with their neighbours over the very land beneath their feet, even as the skies thinned and the waters rose. So when the world drew its breath and the floodwaters settled, the gods declared that from that day, and forever, women were to be subservient to men. They were still needed, though. The population had fallen after the Great Catastrophe, and so women had their uses. There was crude laughter from the men at this that I didn't understand at the time.

When I got home, troubled by the news from the north and the words of the Storyteller, my mother gave me a different version. It was men who had fought wars and made things that were not needed, while the world became hotter and hotter until the great weather systems boiled over and melted the world's ice. She told me great cities were buried beneath the waves around our shores, and that our land once held many more people, until sickness and disease took their toll. Then, carefully checking that my father was not yet heading back and warning my sisters to say nothing, she led me to the Women's House, the secret place the men were not allowed to enter. When I asked Lucas, later, why the men weren't curious about the Women's House, he said it was because they couldn't believe that women might possess anything of value, but he didn't say it unkindly, just as a matter of fact.

My mother led me to the room that housed the sacred books and took one down from the shelf. As she opened it, I saw that the pages were yellowing and the print was fading, but I could make out the lines and lines of black symbols, which she told me were words. She followed them with her eyes and the words that came from her mouth were not her own but those of people – men and women – of a hundred or more years ago. She promised me then, and later kept her promise, that she would teach me the skill of reading, which her mother had taught her, she in turn had been taught by her mother, and so on through the generations. This was how knowledge had been preserved.

'But,' she warned me, 'All who learn this skill are pledged to keep it secret from the men.'

'What?' I was stunned. 'Don't they need to know what's in the books? To make our world better? To stop them from making the same mistakes over and over?'

'Nevertheless. That is the condition.'

'So my father knows nothing of this?' She shook her head.

'And the Headman?' She again shook her head.

I didn't exactly promise, but she assumed the pledge was implicit in my desire to learn, and so the lessons began.

I LOOK BACK now, and wonder what made me so daring, so ready to be different. Perhaps it was because of Lucas. Had I been a boy, I wouldn't have been deemed a fit companion because of my father's lowly status, but as a girl I was unfit twice over. Somehow the double transgression of the norms of our society seemed to cancel each other out in his mind, and so our friendship continued.

When we sat beneath the tables at the feasts, increasingly cramped as our legs grew longer and our heads scraped the underside of the tables, we listened open-mouthed to the stories of how our peaceful world had been destroyed. One night, as the Storyteller was in full flow, I found myself growing angry. By this time, I had read the books, many of them.

'And so the women of the land became greedy. They wanted more and more things, and the men were forced to find ways of getting them, even though it was destroying the land. The women were so powerful that the men feared for their lives...'

'That's not true!' I couldn't stop myself. Lucas clamped a hand firmly across my mouth while putting a finger to his own lips, and then he drew his hand across his throat. I got the message, and nodded my silence.

Afterwards, walking through the shadows so we would not be seen, he asked me why I had said that the stories were not true.

'It says so in the books.'

'What? What books? What are you talking about?'

'Books, books written at the time. The words are in ink. They don't change over time, the way people's spoken words can. They tell a different story.'

I can't blame him for looking disbelieving. He was a

boy. He had been told all his life that women were lesser beings. We parted in silence that night.

It was my determination to prove to him that I knew what I was talking about that led to the reading lessons. He learned quickly, almost as quickly as a girl, and I know I earned his respect as well as his friendship. The shared secret bound us together, but also drove us to distraction.

'Surely everyone should know about this?'

'We'd be locked up before we got the chance to explain.'

It's unjust that women are taking the blame…'

'Will the men give up their power willingly?'

We never reached any conclusion.

THE THREAT FROM the north rumbled on over the years, but nothing ever happened, at least not until the year my father told me it was time for me to marry. I had run from the house with the mark of his hand still livid on my cheek, and his voice ringing in my ears.

'Come back here, useless girl! What else are you good for?'

I ran without awareness of where my feet were taking me. As long as they led me away from him, from the marriage he was eager to force me into, I didn't care. As I grew breathless, I slowed a little. The dark shadows of the forest were starting to close around me. I was still in my apron, a kitchen knife in my pocket. Knives were precious, for the art of tempering steel had been lost, although I had read about it and believed that these ancient skills could be revived.

The cracking of twigs underfoot alerted me to another presence. I tensed, and then relaxed as Lucas emerged from the trees.

'Whoa, steady on. Where are you off to in such a hurry?'

He caught me by the elbows and stilled me, and as I stood, the hairs on my neck stood on end. Over his shoulder I saw the dark shape, taut, drawn back, ready to spring. I heard the low growling in its throat, smelt the fetid odour of its breath…

It was a lucky blow. The knife caught it in just the right part of the throat. I was close enough to see the shock in its yellow eyes, and then it lay, still warm and oozing, at my feet. Fighting down the nausea in my belly, I stooped and cut through a front paw. My mother had certainly kept the knife sharp since her own wolf-killing days.

We entered the centre-space where the men were discussing the news, almost unnoticed. There was a lot of jabbering and gesticulating, and they were all talking over each other. Lucas' father alone stood still at the eye of the storm. In his hand he held a paper, upside down with black markings on it while one of his own spies knelt before him in utter abasement. The Headman saw us. Lucas took that as a sign to approach, and I did the unthinkable and walked beside him into that circle of men.

'May I see?' I held out a trembling hand for the paper. It was good news. The people of the north requested permission to join our settlement. They had crafts and skills to share. I suppose it was a letter – people used to write them so that their words could be carried to others over long distances. As I handed the paper to Lucas I noticed that I had smeared it with blood from the wolf's paw I was still holding.

'Women do kill animals,' I whispered, as he handed the paper to his father. 'When necessary.'

'You must listen to her, Father. She has much to teach us,' he said. Turning to the assembled men, he shouted, 'There will be no war!' and I echoed his words.

'There will be no war.'

One Woman, One Vote

Sallie Anderson

MARY STIRRED HER tea. The spoon clinked against the side of the china cup. William rustled his newspaper once, twice and then again. Ann, the old cook, placed the full toast rack on the polished table between them. She hesitated, as if she was about to say something but didn't. She returned to the kitchen instead.

Mary noted the morning sounds of the house. The clock ticked loudly on the mantle in the sitting room across the hall. Upstairs, Alice was up and her footsteps in her bedroom made the floorboards creak. There was no sound from James' room. He must still be asleep, Mary thought. She supposed that this Saturday in December was no different for her son than any other Saturday. Ann hummed a tuneless melody back in the kitchen. She didn't usually sing. She also didn't usually light a fire at breakfast, but there was no mistaking the warmth coming from the fireplace this morning. Ann was a frugal woman, who ran an efficient, orderly kitchen. Mary listened to the faint hiss of the coals coming from the hearth and thought about the day ahead.

'What time will you go?' William looked at her over the newspaper.

Mary spread butter on her toast and cut it into precise quarters. 'Perhaps after the Ladies' Auxiliary meeting.'

'I'll join you.'

'At the Ladies' Auxiliary meeting?'

'Good God, no.' Her husband snorted. 'I'll accompany you to the polling station.'

Mary slowly chewed a square of toast. Dry crumbs stuck in her throat. 'You're so thoughtful, dear, but I'm sure I can manage. Alice will be with me.'

There was a snort from the other side of the table. 'Mary, I think you underestimate the crowd that will be gathered at the Town Hall. You have no experience in these matters. It's not an appropriate place for our twelve-year old daughter. Especially today. Who knows who will be there? Journalists. Photographers. All kinds of unpleasant people.' He paused. 'Suffragettes.'

While he was talking, Ann entered the room to tend to the fire. William didn't notice but Mary did. 'Thank you, Ann.'

The cook nodded. 'I'll be in the kitchen if you need anything, Mrs. Sullivan.'

Mary spoke softly to her husband when they were alone. 'You're always thinking of our best interests,

William.' She ate another square of toast. This time she swallowed quickly. 'Alice can stay at the house with Ann.'

'Quite right.' He opened and closed the newspaper. He cleared his throat.

'Yes, dear?'

'I want you to vote for the Labour candidate. He was born here. He deserves your first vote.'

'Of course.' Mary poured herself more tea. 'What's his name?'

'Mr. Davison.' He leaned forward. 'This is why women shouldn't have the vote. You don't read the newspaper, dear. You don't understand politics. And why should you? Your concerns are the house and our family.'

'So I rely on you completely to guide me. Who are Mr. Davison's opponents?'

William waved his right hand as if he was shooing away a fly. 'There is only one other name on the ballot. Miss Pankhurst. This whole business has brought shame on the town of Smethwick. The Liberals and Conservatives support her against Mr. Davison. It's outrageous.'

Mary turned the butter knife over in her right hand. She noted the minute brown specks scattered across its buttery edge as she listened to her husband.

'Those Pankhursts are a damned nuisance. If it wasn't for our soldiers coming back from Europe, those ladies wouldn't have got their way.'

'You're spilling your tea, dear.'

William took a deep breath. 'Sensible women like yourself will set a good example at this election.'

A CROWD WAS gathered at the Town Hall. The queue of voters spilled down the steps and along the footpath. Polling officials tried in vain to keep the voters separate from onlookers. Children darted back and forth across the road. Grim Labour party members stood, arms folded, guarding the voters from two energetic women who handed out Women's Party leaflets. A dog tied to the metal railings barked incessantly.

William murmured in Mary's ear, 'I knew it was no place for Alice. I'm sorry you have to stand outside, dear.'

'I'm quite alright.' She pulled up her gloves against the sharp, cold air and let her eyes wander up and down the queue. She recognised many of the women. Some of them were neighbours or members of the Ladies' Auxiliary. She exchanged a nod with the wife of one of William's business partners. Just like Mary, each woman was accompanied by a man: a brother, a husband, a father.

A murmur went up from the crowd. She turned to see two men approach. One held a large camera, the other a notepad and pencil.

William stepped out to block their path. 'What's going on here?'

The man with the notepad smiled, 'Smethwick Echo. Mind if we ask you some questions about today's historic vote?'

'I most certainly do mind.'

The journalist looked over William's shoulder. 'Madam, perhaps you would you like to comment?'

'My wife has no comment.' He shielded her from the men. 'Look away, Mary. We don't want to be on the front cover of tomorrow's paper.'

She did as she was told. She examined the red wall of the Town Hall. Here and there, hairline cracks spread in the mortar between the bricks. It was just like their chimney. Last month, some men came to investigate a leak in the roof. They discovered that the chimney was to blame and set about to fix it. When the men were in the kitchen on a tea break, she overheard them say to Ann, *It's time that does it. Water gets into cracks and makes more cracks. Can't be stopped and best not be ignored or the whole blooming thing comes down.'*

'Mrs. Sullivan!' Mary's thoughts on brickwork were interrupted by a familiar voice. The cook led her young charge through the throng. William looked away. The cook and all things domestic were not his concern.

'I've found you, Mrs. Sullivan. I forgot to buy the roast for tomorrow. Can I...?' The cook's eye widened as she took in the number of women standing in the voting queue. For a moment, she was lost for words.

Mary smiled. 'Yes?'

The cook squared her shoulders and pushed Alice towards her mother. 'The butcher's is busy on a Saturday. It's no place for a young woman like Alice. Can I leave her with you?'

'Of course.' Mary clasped her daughter's small hands between her own and pulled her into the line. William grumbled, but before he could protest, the cook hurried off.

Finally, William and Mary, with Alice squeezed between them, were inside the Town Hall and in the polling station. A man asked Mary to confirm her name and address. William answered for her, accepted both of their ballots and led them towards the row of partitioned polling booths.

'Pardon me.' A young man with a polling clerk badge on his lapel stepped forward. 'Only one person is allowed in a booth at a time.'

'But she's my wife.'

'Sir, it's a secret ballot.'

William's face reddened and he handed one of the ballot papers to his wife. 'Remember what we discussed at breakfast.'

'Yes, dear.' Mary stepped forward with her daughter. The young polling clerk nodded his approval as they both stepped into a booth. Mother and daughter stood together in front of the narrow wooden counter. Mary carefully opened the ballot paper. Alice's fingers slipped between her own to investigate its thin edges and the printed black lettering. So this was what all the fuss was about.

She placed a kiss in Alice's soft brown hair and suppressed the urge to laugh out loud. The ballot was smaller than she expected, but then, she supposed, she had nothing to compare it to. The voting for the Chairwoman of the Ladies' Auxiliary at church was a formality done with a show of hands. This was different. There were two names printed on the ballot: a Mister John Davison and a Miss Christabel Pankhurst. There was a box next to each name. Mary used a stubby, blunt pencil to make a firm cross in one box. Then she carefully folded it in half so her vote was hidden. Before they left the booth, Mary placed the ballot in her daughter's hand and whispered, 'One woman, one vote.'

Cover Their Bright Faces
Abigail Rowe

I CAN SMELL promise in the air as I walk in. It's that tantalising aroma of onions and garlic frying; Linda must be home. I shed my coat and bag, then walk through to the kitchen. The contents of the sauté pan make my mouth water as I lift the lid and inhale. Linda is out on the terrace, favourite mug in hand. Her pre-dinner sencha, no doubt, good woman that she is. I think about pouring a glass of last night's pinot gris, but the pull is too strong. I slide the glass doors open and step out to join her.

'Matty!' She smiles, getting up to embrace me.

I hold her close and bend to kiss the top of her hair, long brown strands catching in my mouth.

She pulls away and looks me in the eye. 'Did you submit the application?'

'Nearly.'

'Nearly means no.' She's laughing but there's that concern flickering across her face.

'The last time a woman was given a senior lectureship was in the nineties. I've no chance… and I just couldn't face handing it to Colin and seeing that effing patronising smirk. Deirdre's back in the admin office tomorrow. I'll hand it in to her.'

'Aw, sweetheart, you can wipe the floor with Colin. Don't mind his smugness.'

I change the subject. 'How was your day?'

'Great, actually. We got a contract for a private function next week, and both baking courses filled up immediately. I think it might be taking off at last.'

'That's brill.' I have no doubt her fledgling business will soar, if Bristol is half the city I think it is. I know I'm biased, but Linda's kitchen skills are phenomenal. 'What's for dinner?'

WE GO BACK inside where Linda tosses tiny tomatoes and herbs into the pan and puts on a huge pot of water for the pasta. I set the table and pour wine. Hands full of fresh linguine pause over the pan.

'Your mum dropped that box round.'

She's not looking at me, so Mum probably wound her up. She has a knack of that, alright, by introducing Linda as 'Matty's friend', or never quite hugging her, tiny slights like that. 'Aunt Portia's stuff? Fab! We can have a root around later.' Linda's now chucking clams into the sauté pan, and twisting the pepper mill ferociously. 'Was she very bad today?'

'Nah. Ignore me. Just the usual killing me with sweetness, you know.'

I do know. We know it could be worse, but it is wearing.

Linda turns, steaming pasta pan in hand fogging up her glasses, and she smiles. 'I love you.'

I laugh as her words make my heart jump and because she can't see a thing anymore. I take the pan from her and pour the contents into the colander while she wipes the steam away.

AFTER DINNER, LINDA works on her spreadsheets so I retrieve the box from the hall and sit on the rug to examine it. An old cardboard box, faded Weetabix logos distorting on its crumpled sides. I only remember Aunt Portia through a child's eyes. She was fusty by the time I appeared; my mother's maiden aunt, tweed and twinset clad, as dry as she was tiny. I know she worked as an archivist, in the British Museum, I think. That suited my child's mind; a relic amongst relics. Mum said she liked my sharp brain, but not my errant ways. 'That means you're naughty,' Mum clarified, though I already knew what errant meant. Aunt Portia was right. I didn't like her any more for that, though.

I peel off the parcel tape and open the box containing all Portia left behind, unlooked at since she died some twenty years ago. A whole life, unexplored, cluttering up an attic. It's half empty, too. On top is an unopened letter postmarked 1998. 'The year she died,' I say out loud.

'Who died? Aunt Portia?' Linda peers from over the screen, forehead wrinkled.

'Yeah, unopened post. Weird to think she never got it.'

I lift out something wrapped in a tired silk neckerchief. A small frame containing an ink-coloured line drawing of a hare, some yellow flowers and downland. Pretty enough. Underneath that are some leather notebooks. I open one and see her close handwriting covering the pages. Apart from the books, there's a hairbrush set and a pile of old letters. I glance through them and see they're all from the same sender, the conferring office of Cambridge University. All twelve say pretty much the same thing.

We note that you completed your degree before 1948. Therefore, regretfully, we are not able to place your name on the honours roll, regardless of your final results.

I don't know what that's about but it was clearly important to Aunt Portia.

Looking through the notebooks, I see diary entries, pretty mundane really: what she was working on, how her plants were coming on, meticulous columns of everything she'd spent that day. *One stamp, 2nd class – 1d. Bus fare 3 1/2d.* And so on. I guess this would be riveting social history in the right hands, but choose to read a slim green volume which has *Memories* inscribed across the flyleaf. A dried flower falls out onto my lap. Virtually colourless, it might have been a cowslip once.

She only roughly sketches her childhood. A house-master's daughter in Harrow. A mousy insignificant child, by her own description. Attending a day school in the town, her sole cosy relationship seems to have been with the headmaster's wife, a Mrs Arbuthnot, who schooled her in Greek and Latin and gave her cocoa. It looks like Portia was itching to leave by the time she started university. I remember that itch well. It tickles me that she felt the same. Then I start to read her Cambridge years. Her stilted tone is still dated but suddenly becomes more fluid.

Whilst Europe began to descend towards darkness, and the Jarrow men trod the long road to London, I walked into the room I was to inhabit for the next three years. I looked around at this vast space that was to be mine. It was divided by a wooden screen into a bedroom area and a study by the window. The porter's boy had placed my trunk in the middle of room. I stood before it for some time, not knowing which way to move. A knock on the door broke my trance. I turned to open it, and there, gazing at me with unabashed curiosity, was Lucy.

'Oh, hello, Lucy!'

'Who's Lucy?' Linda asks, looking more interested now.

'I've only just met her. I'll let you know.' We both giggle.

Linda shuts the laptop and suggests a cup of camomile and honey. I take the journal up to bed, but we don't get any reading done.

DEIRDRE TAKES MY application with alacrity.

'Probably no point, but hey, nothing ventured...' I say.

'No, Matty, you must be in with a shot. You've more research and PhD students under your belt than anyone else.'

'But...'

'But nothing,' she grins, 'and you're way nicer than the others.'

'Pity you're not on the panel.' I blow her a kiss as I leave.

In my office I pick up the green journal again and absorb myself in Portia's life. Two things hit me. She was a brilliant scholar, but not even allowed the status of undergraduate. That's what she calls the male students. I click it must've been a male noun back then. Bloody hell. The other thing is Lucy, her BFF and Girton College soulmate, it seems. Three years and thirty-six pages smattered with Lucy.

> *Lucy, my light and my salvation, so perfectly named. I could not believe that this beautiful creature wanted to be my friend. I thought of Auden, just a few years earlier, sitting and penning That Night When Joy Began. So different, of course, for he writes of a lover, yet apposite. Lucy made the blood flow freer in my veins. I, too, waited for the flash of morning's levelled gun. I grew credulous of peace. She opened my heart and taught me to laugh from the wellspring inside. All my springs are in thee.*

I wish I'd known this Portia. She'd found her niche, and friendship; found life, I guess. I can't even imagine the aunt I knew laughing, let alone feeling joy.

> *So that was Girton: nourishment for the mind, as I was allowed to envelope myself in learning, and for the soul, as I learnt to love and to laugh.*

Her happy tone subsided back to pragmatic retellings after those years. Work as a secretary through the war, and the 50s at the Sorbonne. Completely missing out on all the things that conjures up for me – Simone and Sartre, Jacques Brel, slugging back Pernod, wearing black and chain-smoking *Gauloises sans filtre* on the Left Bank – all that stuff. Nope, not for Portia. She just spent the years translating documents and fending off Frenchmen. I wonder how she lost the luminosity of her Girton years. Was it gradual? Or instantly lost when she left. I get bored once she moves back to London and crack on with some work.

THE DOORBELL RINGS as Linda and I are clearing away the dishes. Mum's standing there, holding some cookery books.

'Is it a good time?' she asks, walking straight through, anyway. 'I've been decluttering again. Good for the mind, apparently. I found these, Linda, wondered if you might like them. Delia recipes never fail.' She puts all three volumes of How to Cook on the kitchen island.

I find myself unable to exhale as I register the dig.

'Your little business might do well to have some old reliables. Not everyone likes the avant-garde, you know.'

'How kind,' says Linda, far more pleasantly than I would have managed. 'I'll put the kettle on. You go through to the front room and have a nice chat with Matty.'

I ask her about Portia, of course. Did she know she'd worked in Paris? Had she ever heard of Lucy?

'Well, she spoke excellent French, so that makes sense. Who is Lucy?'

'A close friend at Cambridge. She's only mentioned one other time in 1946 when Portia writes that Lucy married.'

'They probably lost touch, then. I never knew Portia to have a friend. She preferred talking to pot-plants and antiquities, I think.' Mum's titter rankles.

Linda brings in a tray of tea and excuses herself to work upstairs.

'So how's Dad?' I ask, and pick up the pot to pour.

LATER I LOOK at the framed picture again. It looks like a cheap print. I prise it open and find it's a postcard from The Weald. Postmarked September 1946, it's scrawled:

Merciful Portia,
I'll write properly soon. Very busy.
All my springs,
Lucy

There's some Greek written on a piece of yellowed

paper behind it. I can't make head nor tail of it of course. Linda has the bright idea to scan and search online. That doesn't work.

NEXT DAY, I make my way from the Bio-Science block into the unknown warren of the Classics department. The administrator reminds me of Portia, all stern and po-faced, but she's very helpful and introduces me to a young PhD candidate.

'I know you'll be able to help Matty in a jiffy, Alastair.' She leaves us standing in the corridor.

'Um, sorry about this. I found this in my aunt's be-longings and can't understand it.'

'No problem, let's have a look.' He scans it and looks up straight away. 'Oh, I think I know where this is from. Leave me your email and I'll send you a translation.' He takes his phone and snaps a shot of it.

'Thank you so much,' I say, left standing with the scrap of Portia's life in my hands.

When I get back to the office, Colin is there.

'That's a stellar application you submitted, Matilda,' he says, with no side to his words. I'm taken aback and smile my thanks. Maybe... just maybe I have a chance.

I GET THE email from Alastair that evening. Linda finds

me on the sofa with in tears.

'What's wrong, love?' She puts her arms round me.

'Nothing!' I say. 'It's beautiful. It's Sappho.' I show her the translation.

Awed by her splendour
stars near the lovely
moon cover their own
bright faces
when she
is roundest and lights
earth with her silver.

'Oh, poor, poor Portia.' Linda says, 'She was in love.'

'I don't know if she even knew it,' I sob.

'We do,' Linda says and kisses my wet cheeks.

She's right. We live the promise that Portia only scented. I make a vow to live it for her, too.

I PHONE MUM to find out where Portia is buried, and Linda and I make plans. We make a day trip of it, drive to Berkshire and find the churchyard. She's there, under an oak, and a headstone that wastes no words.

Portia Beausang, 11/12/1918 – 22/05/1998

We plant cowslips on the plot and Linda hands me the letter that arrived the week she died. I read it out.

Dear Ms Beausang,

As one of our alumni of 1939, we are delighted to invite you to come to your conferring ceremony on Saturday, 4th July, 1998, on which day your name will be placed upon the roll of honours graduates. The day will be a celebration of the 900 women who completed prior to 1948. Please see the information sheet for further information and RSVP procedures.

We hope you are able to attend.

Yours sincerely,
Angela Williams
Senior Administrator, Girton College

'Congratulations, Portia Beausang, Batchelor of Arts, First Class with Honours'. I tuck the letter in the cleft between the soil and the headstone, then pull Linda forward.

'This is Linda,' I say. 'She lights my earth, like your Lucy did for you. Nowadays we show our bright faces, and it's okay.'

We stay a while, peaceful in the dappled light.

On the drive home Mum phones to wish me luck for the interview tomorrow. I tell her nothing of our day. It's ours, and Portia's, and it shines.

My Mother Left Me For A Tree
Rosaleen Lynch

MY MOTHER LEFT me for a tree. Most people I knew knew this, but how they interpreted the knowledge I didn't know. A tree? You'd think that would be the first question. Most people think that they've heard me wrong or got the wrong end of the stick. I didn't mean that as a joke, but it does say what I mean.

How could someone leave their child? That was usually the first question from people who had come from an 'unbroken' family. Why did 'she' leave and not your dad? That was the usual question from products of a 'broken' family. Or do you have two mums? Next come the placatory strokes meant to raise my confidence in myself, dispense with blame culture and promote healing. I could go into them but that would serve no purpose. And it was too late for any good. They could throw all the shite they liked at me but no amount of fertilizer was going to make me grow any more.

I was four when my mother left me for a tree. I accepted that it was a good enough reason. A tree. They seemed pretty important and a tree couldn't move in with us so she had no choice, I thought.

And no it was not a 'family tree' or the 'tree of knowledge' or a special tree in a conservation area that my mother climbed into to save a forest from a bulldozer. It was just a tree. With branches and leaves and rings to tell its age.

My therapist tried to dig further, to the roots of it all, you might say. She said anyway. We talked about tree surgeons and tree huggers and what if it wasn't a tree but part of the name of someone like Roger Daltry. I listened to her ideas but respectfully declined to entertain any ideas relating to my mother having a relationship with Roger Daltry or anyone else with the sound of 'tree' in their name. There was even the suggestion that the soft Irish pronunciation of the number 'three' was a possibility. But I knew the difference between when my mother said 'tree' and 'three'. I knew that however strong my mother's accent was, she didn't move into number three of any-house anywhere. That much I knew. Other 'tree' ending words were discussed but my mother was not in the Irish town of Bantry. And though it was a joke, I was not impressed, when the one I was once going to marry, said it was a mystery. The end of the word 'mystery' is 'tery' not 'tree' I told my then fiancée. That wasn't the reason we didn't marry. My therapist blamed my mother.

I reasoned that that was impossible seeing as she wasn't around to take the blame. I talked instead to my therapist of the aptness of 'forestry' ending in the sound of 'tree' and how in a metaphor my mother could have, just as easily, left me for poetry.

I could tell my therapist wasn't happy. She seemed to want to make sense of it more than I did. I found out from a neighbour that she had been adopted, my therapist not my neighbour. That made sense.

The reason my mother left did not bother me. No more than the reason that the 'tree' sound in a word like 'chemistry' sounded different on its own. Try. It was not the same unaccompanied and knowing why didn't matter. Memories weren't made of whys. Mine were set to music, like the subconscious soundtrack of my life. Nursery rhymes grew to anthems and they drained into sad love songs and the kind of classical music that funerals were known for. My mother's music came from the radio. It was tuned to love and loss, pain and sorrow, and ideas I had yet to understand like paving paradise and putting trees in tree museums. Often, in moving the radio to the back garden the dial was knocked and came to rest on the edge of a frequency, crackling in and out of transmission. The antennae then needed to be moved to point to a particular area in the sky to pick up the radio station while trying to settle the dial, then adjust the antenna again, as if waiting for a message to come on a frequency from another world. A universe outside our garden, asking us where all the flowers had gone and telling us that all the leaves were brown and that the answer was blowing in the wind.

I once climbed my mother's legs into her arms, her brown corduroy bell-bottom jeans, long and planted in the ground below me, her arms a paisley green around me. She wore flowers in her hair and plucked one out to put in mine. She might have smiled but the sun blinded me so I couldn't tell, all I could see were leaves around us and I felt so far up off the ground. She was taller than she became.

Her smell was either of lavender oil or the turquoise bottled eau de cologne her mother gave her. Elastic bands snapped on her wrists as reminders and were used for securing posters, paintings or pages, in rolls. She left cardboard boxes unpacked and tea chests of books for mice to bed in. The only book I ever saw her read was *To the Lighthouse*. I didn't read it until my therapist said I should. Should people take reading recommendations from their shrinks? I learned nothing from it, apart from confirmation that Virginia Woolf was a good writer. And there were references to mothers and daughters that I would never understand. Some lines were marked, in my mother's copy. That, of course, the therapist was interested in. One line was about the character of an artist who thought of rearranging the scene in front of her to be more to her liking. 'She would move the tree rather more to the middle,' it read. I wondered if she meant to move the actual tree, her perspective of the tree or the tree in the painting. All had their advantages, I thought. And later, there were the following lines:

'And all the lives we ever lived.

And all the lives to be.

Are full of trees and changing leaves.'

My therapist thought it was a sign. And although it was a surprise when my mother returned again, I didn't think anyone attributed it to the words of Virginia Woolf. Nor could I imagine those words to have been the cause of her leaving. I am a great non-believer in fate and a strong believer in coincidence. Yes, apples don't fall far from the tree but if they are picked and the seeds sown elsewhere they can grow up in a very different climate across the world.

I have a tree in my garden. My mother comes to visit it. She doesn't say she does but she will always remark on its situation. The foliage. The weather. The flowers and seeds. We might be in the kitchen looking out at the wind whipping through the leaves or the way the snow lies on the horizontal or catches where the branches meet the trunk. Or we might be in the garden sunshine splayed out under its shade.

My mother will move in with me when she can no longer look after herself. She wondered how I could say I'd take her in, when she had left me for a tree. I told her I knew she had no choice, what would a tree do without her? She asked me if I'd bought the house because the garden had a tree. No, I said, I bought the house unseen but decided to live in it when I saw the tree, not even knowing then if it was apple or cherry blossom. And on an impulse I rarely had, I bought the house next door because there was no tree, so mine would have room to grow, the roots able to stretch out under the earth into the other garden. I thought I might even knock down that other house and grow more trees. Let the earth return to forest.

My mother is sitting under the tree now, eyes closed and face upturned, basking in the dappled light.

I wonder if I could bury her there, if she would be good for the tree?

What is the wrong end of a stick?

Myopia

Sophie Duffy

IT WAS ONE of those dull afternoons, mid-week, mid-November, dark already, the tea things cleared away but too soon to be thinking about supper. Richard had telephoned to say he would be late, but Laura wasn't alone; she had her sister Betty here to stay.

Dear Betty.

The pair of them sat by the fire in the drawing room, the wireless on. Betty was turning the heel of a sock. Laura should be darning her husband's socks but her eyesight couldn't manage such small delicate tasks unless she had daylight to see by. So she sat idle-handed, glancing at a well-used copy of *Good Housekeeping*. Articles, adverts, advice. Housing, budgeting, nutrition. Tide, Vim, Vinolia Baby Soap. *Pay up, save up, chin up! Turn out your ragbag: it may make a glad bag. Your child can't decide to be immunised.*

What use was any of this to her now? She'd done all of those things, taken all that advice, used all those products. Her house was clean, her National Savings were topped up, her daughters were adults, living in digs in Central London, one of them engaged, the other up to goodness knew what.

'Heavens, Laura.' Betty lay aside the sock, peering over her glasses with their mother's pale blue eyes. 'Whatever's the matter?'

'Nothing's the matter.' She heard herself snap like one of those disappointing indoor fireworks her girls had egged Richard to buy one New Year many moons ago.

'Then why on earth are you sighing so much?'

'I wasn't aware that I was?'

'You were.' Betty gave her the look that older sister's share so willingly. 'Come on, dear. You can tell all. You know me, I don't judge.'

The thing was, Betty did judge. A tut when she saw a baby with a dummy in its mouth. A shake of the head when fingering a layer of dust on the spindles of the stairs. A recipe for corned beef hash cut neatly from her *Woman's Realm* and slipped between the pages of Laura's diary.

'I'm simply tired, that's all.' Laura inhaled deeply. 'Nothing to worry about.' Another breath. 'Sorry if I was getting on your nerves.'

'No, dear. My nerves are like steel. Yours on the other hand…'

'On the other hand?'

'Well, Laura, you are quite renowned for your nerves.' The knitting needles clattered. 'You were always the sensitive one. Hence Mother's softly-softly approach with you.'

Laura flicked over the page to avoid another sigh, but it was all she could do to hold it in while confronted for an advert for a woman's electric shaver. Whatever next? As if Richard would care about the smoothness of her legs.

Her sister was right of course. Laura's nerves were renowned amongst older relatives who could remember her anxieties as a child. She'd seen tragedies all around. Everywhere she looked there was a disaster on the verge of happening. A dog charging out into the road. A child letting go of her mother's hand. A drunk swaying too near the platform edge. Becoming an adult hadn't helped. Being a mother meant she now fretted about her own children. Each tear, each cough, each cut knee was enough to bring on cold sweats, despite having a doctor for a husband, one that didn't have to join up because he was needed at home. Despite his reassuring efforts, she was convinced each malady would end in premature death.

But, funnily enough, the war changed all that. The war strengthened her. Yes, there were moments of terror, of course there were, but her nearest and dearest somehow came out the other end unscathed. Despite remaining in Croydon for the duration, they suffered only a few broken windows and the odd bump and bruise from stumbling around in the blackout. Every day that passed gave Laura courage. Every night endured gave her hope. Her stoicism took the aunts quite by surprise. And her mother. And Betty. Especially Richard.

On clattered the needles. The wireless crackled. The fire spat.

The war.

It was the most exciting time of Laura's life; she'd been needed for more than clean handkerchiefs.

Now it was over. The future was supposed to be bright. But despite a new government, a new national health service, the drudgery of rationing had worsened and the heartache of loss deepened. Not loss of lives but rather the loss of *her* life.

'Let me get supper, Laura,' Betty cajoled. 'You go up and have a bath. You'll feel much brighter after that and Richard will be so pleased to see a glow in your cheeks.'

The nerves were creeping back, the little Nazis.

SHE LAY IN the bath, submerged and warm. It was a luxury she'd barely had time to miss during those crucial months when the tide began to turn. Richard hadn't been all that keen on her taking up a job at the war office but she couldn't bear to continue as a WVS volunteer, admirable as those women had been – still were, if her sister was anything to go by.

She'd got the job by chance – an encounter at a cocktail party. A contact was made. A phone call followed. Then a trek up to town for an interview and, before she could think too deeply about it, she was signing the Official Secrets Act. It was all so very hush-hush. So very exhilarating. The commute that could take hours depending on the raids. The work. The colleagues. Her boss who was high up in the Admiralty. The brown files, the rushing up and down of corridors. And the money! She had her own money. Not much but it was hers.

Now all that remained was her housekeeping and a very small bond from her grandmother. Not forgetting those wretched National Savings.

She lay in the bath until the water was tepid and Betty was rattling the door handle.

LATER, WRAPPED IN her dressing gown, her hair caught up in a turban, she sat with her sister at the kitchen table.

'You have Richard, my dear,' Betty told her, as if she didn't know. 'He's a wonderful husband. And two super girls who will soon settle down to married life. That's all a mother can ask of her daughters.'

Was that all one could hope for one's daughters? They had jobs now. They had excitement. But Polly had got engaged. She'd have to give up her work when she married. She could only pray that Georgina would not find love for a very long time.

'Must we always choose, Betty?'

'Choose what, dear?' Betty busied herself scraping the last of an egg white out of its shell. 'Do eat up. You've hardly touched your bread and butter.'

Laura ate up but she felt queasy and unsettled. Where was Richard?

IT WAS PAST half past nine by the time Richard came home, pale and harassed.

Betty fussed around her beloved brother-in-law, making him supper and cocoa. Laura sat with them at the kitchen table but all she could see were the empty chairs where her children used to sit. The boiled eggs they had decapitated. The jam sandwiches they'd demolished. The meals they'd shared as a family before the war.

Betty prattled on ... Mr Attlee... the scarcity of decent tea ... the price of brisket...

She could cry but she must pull herself together. She'd lost her job, not her life, or Richard's, or Polly's or Georgina's. That's what Betty kept on reminding her.

'If only you could knit or sew,' Betty said later, heading up the stairs to bed with the dratted *Good Housekeeping* clutched to her bosom. 'It would be so much healthier to occupy yourself with something useful.'

'I used to do something useful.' She hated the sound of her own voice, so piteous and wimpish.

'Now, dear, it's no good looking backwards.' Betty stood at her bedroom door, more and more like their mother. 'Those dark days are gone, thank heavens.'

Dear Betty.

THE NEXT DAY brought rain. This was not enough to deter Betty from taking her to the shops, armed with a basket and a battered old umbrella with wonky spokes. After they'd bought the daily provisions, Laura suggested a visit to the tea shop on the corner. Betty examined her with those pale blue eyes. Did she suspect her younger sister of gluttony? Profligacy? Degeneracy? Whatever it was, Betty was determined not to enter that den of iniquity, and was now propelling Laura in the other direction.

'Where are we going, Betty? You're hurting my arm.'

'Don't fuss, Laura. All will be revealed.'

THE DOOR BELL of the optician's pinged as Laura was nudged over the threshold. The sisters stood side by side in a gathering pool of dampness while an earnest assistant with heavy pebble-stoned spectacles enquired as to their business.

'My sister needs an eye examination.'

'You've come to the right place.' The woman smiled; Laura's shoulders relaxed somewhat. 'Do sit yourself down.'

Laura did as she was told, Betty plonking herself next to her, and gave the woman the details she requested. Yes, reading small print was becoming troublesome. No, she hadn't had a test for a while. Yes, perhaps she ought to have an examination soon.

'I have some time now?' the woman said.

'Pardon?'

'To do the test.'

'You do?'

'I'm the optician.' The woman laughed. 'My receptionist is visiting her poorly mother. Again. So I'm manning the fort, as it were.'

'Oh, right, I see. Of course, yes.' Laura felt a blush creeping over her face, realisation striking. This woman was the optician. Goodness. The assumptions one made, after everything she'd been through.

She really did need glasses. Maybe then she'd see more clearly.

BETTY WAS STILL ensconced in the spare bedroom the following week when Laura received a telephone call to say the glasses were ready and would she pop in and have them fitted. Betty insisted on accompanying her – she wanted to get some more wool. Betty's knitting bag was full of yarn but Laura didn't mind. She realised her sister needed her as much as she needed her sister.

The frames were tortoiseshell. The lenses clean and sparkling. And Laura could read the tiny print on the optician's card, right to the bottom of the page. It was quite miraculous.

Laura splashed out on some wool too. She'd like to try turning a heel and make some socks for Richard for Christmas. He'd be so impressed.

IT WAS HOPELESS. She might be able to see the stitches but they were in the wrong place and holes gaped like missing teeth. The sock was a tangled, sweaty mess. She couldn't ask Betty for help because she'd gone home the previous day, clutching her suitcase and basket with packed lunch for the journey. Back to Reigate and her pompous husband. Her WVS. Her busy, ordered life.

Oh, it was no good. She'd have to buy Richard the wretched socks from the Army and Navy. She shoved the pathetic creation and the blasted needles back into the patchwork bag that Betty had whipped up as a parting gift (dear Betty) and felt thoroughly miserable.

What was she to do instead? The daily had been in and swept and dusted. She herself had polished the brass and silver. Groceries had been queued for and bought. She would just have to sit on the window seat and read. Not the tatty magazines but the local paper. The two minute wonder. She might learn something, improve her mind. With her specs arranged carefully across the bridge of her nose, she embarked on this new education. Unfortunately, not much information could be gleaned: The date and venue of the next church jumble. The rugger results of the local half-rate public school. The usual articles, adverts, and advice. But, towards the back, Situations Vacant. A job in the optician's. Training provided.

She went directly to the bureau, took out her best pre-war paper and an envelope and began to write.

THE SUN WAS being brave for November. She'd dash out right this minute to catch the post. She could wait for the morning and deliver it personally, save a stamp, but this seemed more appropriate. Official. Important.

She put on her coat and scarf, held the letter in her gloved hand, like a precious, urgent message, like the memoranda she used to rush along the corridors of power for her Admiral. Down the garden path, the leaves piling up since Betty's departure and the gusty short days. Along the pavement to the corner, a step off the kerb into the road, heading for the pillar box on the other side.

Halfway across, a movement flashed in the corner of her eye. A frantic ring of a bell and the deep gravelly torrent of swear words from the normally gently-spoken postman.

He stopped just in time.

'You need your eyesight checking, Mrs Peters,' he said, doffing his cap to make up for his dirty mouth.

She smiled at him. 'I'm sorry,' she said. 'But don't worry. I've got it in hand.'

She felt him stare after her as she walked purposefully to the far pavement. She waited by the pillar box as he wheeled his bike to where the park used to have railings and propped it against a tree stump. He emptied the post into his sack and she handed him her own letter to add to the collection. He nodded good evening and went on his way. She stayed awhile, watching him disappear round the corner of the park.

As she walked home, she thought about what she would get Richard for supper. She thought about her daughters and their plans for Christmas. She thought about her tortoiseshell glasses with their sparkling lenses. The specs would not only help her to read, but they might also enable her to head off disaster. Then again, they might not. Today she'd managed on her instincts. She'd survived. But nothing was certain; one lived in a world of chaos. One must get through each hour of each day, each hour of each night. All one could do was be resolute.

One must go on. Because, when one really thought about it, why weren't there more crashes? Why weren't there more accidents? More death? More genocide? More evil?

Something beyond control made the earth keep turning, the sun rise and set. All she could really do was hang on, dig deep, try her hardest. She could see it all so clearly now.

Chin up!

The Colour Of Sunflowers

Kate Vine

Monday

THE MORNING COMES with plans. They are complete and fully functional. The kind you make in January. Clean and fresh. I would get up at 6.30am and write poetry – just a few lines, just for me, lines that would draw things together and put them in order. I would then take a walk, buy breakfast at the market. It would be easy. Peaceful.

Instead I sleep until noon. Hours and hours spent drifting. Avoiding the moment when I truly wake – the moment I remember. There's always a slip of a second when I know nothing. Who I am, what has been before. But then the memories come.

They are not the memories I'd expect; I relive not the night it happened but the times before. The expression on his face when I brought him coffee. His hand on my shoulder as he passed my desk. That blue, striped shirt he wore. They come together, these memories, and form one voice – a voice that's not even his.

A voice that says *You should have known.*

A voice that says *It's all your fault.*

There is one week left before the trial. I have decided to spend it alone.

***

AT THE MARKET I meet a man who looks like a sparrow. He is standing by the fruit stall.

'What is that?' he says, pointing.

'A dragon fruit,' I say. 'Or a pitaya.' Its shell is vibrant pink, with lime green claws. But inside is the white of fresh snow.

'Do you eat it raw?'

'You can,' I reply.

The stallholder listens. She is a small woman, with wide, low breasts.

'Two for three pounds,' she says.

The man picks one up. He rolls it in his hand, feeling its texture.

'Why don't we get one each?' he asks. His hairline is receding, deep lines furrow his forehead.

I look at the woman and then back at him. They wait.

'No, thank you,' I say.

'It's a good price!' the woman says. Her accent is strange, her vowels twisted.

'I'm sorry,' I say.

'It's a bargain!' the man says, even though he only just

learned of the fruit's existence. 'Go on, only one fifty each.'

He starts scrabbling in his jeans pocket for coins. When he passes them to me, his skin presses mine and a noise escapes my mouth. I leap away, the coins splattering across the pavement.

'I'm sorry,' I repeat.

They both start to speak but I can't make out the words. I leave abruptly, without a dragon fruit. Or a pitaya.

Tuesday

I WAKE SUDDENLY to rain thrashing against my window. It takes half an hour for my heart rate to slow. I keep dark chocolate on my bedside table, as bitter as I can bear, and I suck chunks of it as I try to breathe.

The rain has no thought for rhythm; it is angry, fevered. I wonder if I can harness its force, hold it in my chest. Ready for when I need it.

***

I WEAR A heavy sweatshirt with my jeans and I walk along the Thames path. I like how the London water makes no attempts at beauty; it is unashamedly grey, filth floating on its surface. Sometimes people jump from the bridges into its void. I imagine bones cracking, spines smashing into splinters. My mother asks me to stay away from the river. She fears I too will jump. But that's not what I wish for. I wish only for clean surfaces, an untouched table cloth.

***

THE LAWYER CALLS at three o'clock about a witness. Mrs Rawson, he says, she worked in the building opposite. I nod even though he can't see me. I don't know Mrs Rawson, nor why she has only come forward now.

I suppose she must have worries of her own. I struggle to imagine what other people are anxious about. My mother looks at me sometimes, the strain thick on her face, and I want to care.

But I can't.

Wednesday

IT RAINS AGAIN today, this time in softer strikes. If I could, I'd think about my old boyfriend's arms, the way they would fold around me, enveloping me in his gentle smell. But it's too hard to think of him without thinking of those other arms, other hands. They get confused.

At the bookshop I buy a poetry anthology. The cover is blue and smooth; it feels solid in my hands. One piece is about the bees that live in a woman's garden. Her house, the hive, they begin to merge and this scares me. I need barriers. I long for armour.

I sit down on the bookshop sofa.

'Are you alright?' a woman asks.

She looks down and I see my fingernails are driving into my knees. There is hot pain in my skin, yet I cannot let go.

The woman sits down beside me, breathing out a long sigh.

'I'm sorry,' I say. My knees begin to shake and I hold on even tighter. I imagine the marks forming where my nails dig in, deep and hard. I can see she wants to help but if she touches me I will scream.

'Is there someone I can call?' she says.

'No,' I say. My mum can't touch me either. 'Don't worry. It'll pass.'

The woman smiles. 'Everything does.'

Thursday

WHAT HAPPENED TO me is *unjust*, the lawyer says. I write that word down so many times it loses all meaning.

I search for something different. Colours, words. I don't know whether it was dark or I simply couldn't see.

I make a list.

Darkness.

Him.

Black.

Him.

Mine. Not. His.

I read again about the bees. The woman starts to hear a soft buzzing wherever she goes. It follows her into her dreams.

Some nights I dream that I stitch my thighs together.

***

MY MOTHER CALLS. I tell her she can't come round. *This week is important*, I say. She tries to understand.

Friday

THE SUN IS warm and I walk to the Common. Groups of young people lounge on blankets drinking cans of beer. Children enter the park in pairs, holding hands with one another. The teacher tips her face to the sun, her eyes tired.

I sit on a bench with my notebook. Every strand of grass is the same shade of green. My knees are still sore and scabbed from the bookshop but, in some ways, it is pleasurable. I stroke my fingertips over the jagged grooves and I love that I made my mark.

Hope. I write it down – once, twice, three times. It feels sour and pungent. Right, now I have hope – see? It is there on the page. I've learned not to hope for quietness, or redemption. But I still hope for justice. If he is punished, maybe I no longer will be.

The lawyer says they might not have enough to con-vict.

You didn't say no, he says.

She didn't say yes, my mother says.

I stare at the clusters of young people. They seem part of a different world. The men, they stand up, they stretch, they play football; the women lie down and watch. Some wear bikini tops and very short shorts. I want to yell at them, tell them to get up, to run while they still can – *feel the heat of your own sweat*. But my cries are silent.

He knew what I didn't. That I was lonely.

***

WHATEVER YOU DO, don't blame yourself, the lawyer says. *The defence will do that for you.*

***

THE LAWYER CALLS again.

'There's been a case in Birmingham,' he says. 'Very similar circumstances. Abuse of power.'

'A boss?'

'A CEO. He got eight years.'

'That's good?'

'That's what we're aiming for.'

I wonder if in eight years' time I will be free.

'This is good news,' he says.

In bed that night I open my notebook.

Hope.

Hope.

Hope.

I tear it from the book and throw it across the room.

Saturday

I FIND THE piece of paper and pin it to my wall.

Sunday

MY HEART SIMMERS. I scratch my knees. I consider peeling away the scabs and pressing my fingers into the raw flesh. I want to find out how much pain I can take.

I think about what I should wear tomorrow. It is a mathematical equation – no, an *optical illusion*. I write that down.

The lawyer told me to dress very carefully. *Nothing too short*, he says. *Nothing too sheer. Those shoes are too high.*

You can borrow mine, my mother says.

I find a dress that reaches my knees and covers my shoulders. It is a deep shade of navy, the kind that looks black in certain light. I tie my hair back and look in the mirror, try to recognise myself. What words could explain my body?

My finger prints are dotted down the glass. I haven't cleaned the mirror since I moved in two years ago. I suppose it is now a relic. Traces of who I used to be.

***

I WANT TO find the colour of this story. It has the darkness of black, the heat of red. The confusion of turquoise, neither one thing nor another. But these colours, they have beauty and there is nothing beautiful about this. It is the murky grey-brown of the Thames, thick with the rotting bones of those who could not push on.

I see my note, hanging from my wall. What is the colour of hope? I imagine a rainbow, a fresh streak across the London sky. A *spectrum*.

In my wardrobe is a different dress. This one is sleeveless and has pockets at the hips. I wore it one day last June when my boyfriend held my hand and told me I smelled of summer.

The dress is yellow and bold. Hope, I decide, is the colour of sunflowers.

***

I CURL UNDER my covers and try to close my eyes. Words flash beneath my lids.

Tomorrow.

Tomorrow.

Him.

Tomorrow.

I push my fingernails into my palms. I will be there in the courtroom – I'm told it's more effective. But I also want to see his face again. Make a new memory. One that I decided to make.

Tomorrow.

My yellow dress hangs on my wardrobe door ready for me. In its pocket is my note.

Hope.

Hope.

Hope.

I'm going to carry it with me. Hold it in my hand. He can't take it from me.

When the dawn crests, I step slowly from my bed. Wipe my eyes. It is early but I enjoy these moments of stillness, before the city reignites. I watch the light rise over the rooftops.

I take the note from the pocket and grab my pen. Scratch one more word.

Sunflowers.

I put it back in. And I am ready.

Enid Is Going On A Journey

David Cook

WINDOWS DOWN, THE old red Escort wound its way around the labyrinthine country lanes. Enid jabbed a finger at the CD player and winced as trumpets oompah-ed in her ears.

'I'm driving, so we listen to my music,' Steven had always said, when he was at the wheel.

She pressed eject and hurled the disc of brass band classics from the car, almost decapitating a nearby thrush. She fiddled with the radio until she heard Dusty Spring-field singing about how she was only twenty-four hours from Tulsa. Maybe one day Enid would visit Tulsa. She liked the sound of that. But not yet. Bournemouth first.

'Can't stand beaches. What do you want to go away for, anyway? Haven't you got everything you need right here?'

She hummed along, admiring the cottages that looked so much like the ones in the playsets she'd had as a young girl, back when her horizon seemed limitless and she might go anywhere and do anything. Then she'd married Steven and found that, actually, her horizon stopped at the kitchen door.

'Let's just get where we're going. They built motorways so people didn't have to drive through tinpot villages. The countryside stinks of cow shit anyway.'

ENID INHALED. SURE enough, there was a stench of faeces in the air. It smelled like the freedom she'd craved for so long. This craving had grown so strong over the last decade of marriage that last year she'd finally plucked up the courage to ask for a little independence of her own.

'DRIVING LESSONS? YOU? At your age? You already drive me up the wall, isn't that enough?'

And that had been the final straw as far as Enid was concerned. She'd saved up her pension until she could afford a driving instructor, who'd taught her three point turns and clutch control while Steven was out frittering away money at the greyhound track. But although there was a little cash left over, she couldn't stretch to a car as well. That was why she'd had to sneak out early this morning with a suitcase, nabbing Steven's keys from the kitchen table as she left. He'd be raising hell at home, but that didn't matter because she was never going there again. It wasn't as if he'd call the police. Tell them his little old wife had made off with his car? He'd be too ashamed to admit such a loss of control over her.

THE COTTAGES DISAPPEARED in her rear view mirror. Enid put her foot on the accelerator. The beach was waiting.

To The Sea

Helen Irene Young

WE'D NEVER MEANT to travel in a convoy. Dad didn't like group trips, preferring to holiday with just Mum and us two kids, managed through the child safety-lock system in the back of our Ford Escort. This trip was something different. Mum knew it and so did I, and that was exciting for us. It was something he couldn't control. The other car, for example, might want extra toilet breaks or 'breathers' as Mum called them when she argued with him for one of her own on past outings. Stopping was akin to militancy. Dad would have hit his destination in a single gulp if he could have. Of course, we did stop, so that he could smoke. When the idea for a two-car convoy had been set in motion, I could already see him thinking about that, wondering if he could do without the smoking this one time. Imagine, if we stopped and every person in the other car got out? I thought about it too. Mostly, about how refreshing it would be to do something differently.

I'd never travelled with the family in the other car, despite being close friends with the eldest girl, Claire. They were very outdoorsy and this made me see them as people separate from their car, as much as we were integral to ours. I could sense that getting there didn't seem to matter to them as it did to us. I knew that Dad sensed this too. I didn't altogether like our way of travelling. It was just what I was used to. Sometimes I got hungry when we travelled and stressed by all the rowing going on in the front of the car. I had already decided at home as I packed, that these extra stops, when they came, would be a good thing for our family. I'd already set myself up to enjoy them. I was anxious for Dad though, I hoped he wouldn't cause a scene in front of the other car. That he could cope with change this one time and that it wouldn't spoil the whole trip. I hoped it wouldn't reveal something about him and, through association, about us. It was only a weekend camping trip after all. Yet, our car had never been camping before. That was a problem in itself and Mum, Dad and I knew it. My baby brother was outside this sphere of concern because he was still a baby and completely made-up by any experience he saw as new.

For Dad, travelling meant arriving at his destination. It meant being as far away from where he had come from as it was possible to get – as though he was afraid that at any moment he would be sucked back into his actual life by some external force. At this time, he worked in a large factory making cable for commercial aeroplanes. He had split cable and run it through machines for eleven years, which is how old I was then. With this trip, as with the ones before it, he intended to place as many miles between himself and that cable production line as were possible to get. He called the place he worked 'The Tomb'. He told me it was called this in one of our father–daughter moments in which he treated me like a confidante. He would tell me just how disappointed by life he was and I would listen and pretend to understand, even though my inexperience meant I wasn't really able to empathise beyond my own needs. I was always left unfathomably depressed by these exchanges and convinced that he must in some way be disappointed with us, his family, too.

For his part, he was convinced that he would die if he stayed working there. Something had happened before I was born that concerned the purchase of our council house during the Thatcher era. This house had been my mother's house as a child and so this meant he blamed her as well as the last prime minister for this early death by cable making. My mother was frustrated with life in her own way, probably more so than him, but she never spoke to me about it. Many years later, she died of a cataclysmic brain tumour, which could in part have been due to her not talking about things. But that came later. On this trip we were immune to death.

We left the beige suburban brickwork of my hometown far behind. Only then was I able to pick over the idea of us camping instead. The problem with the camping trip was that we weren't the type of family who stayed outdoors overnight. In the front seat I could see Dad thinking this too. My parents had been pushed into the trip by Claire's parents, and by me. At this time in my life, I secretly wished I was in the other car, permanently. I thought the other car-people were my kind of car-people. Sometimes, I went as far as fantasising about being adopted by them, but I'd never have gone through with it. Unfortunately, I loved my family.

That summer I was in a rebellious mood. It all went back to what had happened two months previously, when my parents had forbidden me from attending the Brownie Guide camping trip – the one where all the district packs get together to pitch tents and toast marshmallows. Mum hadn't wanted me to go because she had a child's fear of enclosed wooded spaces born of fairy-tales. She had convinced Dad I might go missing. At Brownies, I had risen to Sixer but was no one if I hadn't toasted marsh-mallows in the New Forest. After the trip, when everyone came back bonded and accounted for, the damage had already been done. She had made an outsider of me then. On reflection, it was one of those childhood disappoint-ments that have the potential to harden a young soul into adulthood, although I wasn't emotionally developed enough to realise this then. What I did know, is that my parents owed me. I could tell Mum and Dad were nervous about camping, but I remember thinking (in an act of generosity that surprised me), that it would be good for them.

The journey to the campsite took most of the day and as it turned out, we only stopped once, when both car-dads got out to smoke. Us kids and the mums also got out but hung about the two cars, Claire and I peering in at each other's travelling space as though we had any control over the amount of camping junk packed in around us. I was the winner on this account because I only had to share with a baby in a car seat and the frame of his travel cot. My family didn't own any camping stuff anyway but I only realised it when I saw her looking into our car window for it. It was as though all that space meant I lacked other things too.

No one went into the service station for refreshments, we had hot squashed sandwiches which we planned to gobble on the motorway, and so we all climbed back in again once the smoking was done. The nicotine had loosened my father up marvellously so that when we slipped into Dorset things were as I imagined they were in the other car, easy and polite. Claire's dad was ahead of us by this point. It had to be this way because this car had been to the campsite before and knew where it was going. I sensed that my dad didn't like this because he had lots to say about the driving of the car in front.

'I know how to drive,' he kept saying, as though following this other car was a form of submission that suggested he wasn't really driving at all.

From the back seat I watched him side-on. I could see him working out the consequences of what might happen if he stopped following the car in front and how this might be explained later when we all met again at the campsite. His face got progressively redder.

'Calm down,' my mother said.

'I know how to drive!' he replied, as though what she'd really said was 'In a competition between you and him, he would win.'

My father lost it. Losing it meant an increase in speed because for him speed meant power. It came as no surprise to me that we quickly overtook the car in front. My mum coughed. We both knew this wasn't part of the plan. I turned my head sideways so that I might see Claire as I sped past her. Ah, Claire who had been allowed on the Brownie camping trip. For a moment I was with him. Like father like daughter. I basked in the short-lived glory of it – this notion that all good things arrive first. I found her face squashed up against the window, asleep. Instead, I locked eyes with her father. His said: I don't understand what your car is doing.

He looked concerned for us and I knew then that this concern extended only to my mum, my brother and me.

With my eyes, I tried to convey a look that suggested I'd just met my dad. For me, adoption was back on the table. It was all the gesture I had time for as we were shunted back onto the correct side of the road, leaving the other car behind us. In the front, my mum coughed again.

'You bloody idiot. You don't know where you're going,' she said.

It was dark by the time we reached the campsite. The absence of light was a problem because we had never put up a tent before. I owned a Wendy house as a child but my uncle built that. It had started to rain. Dad got out of the car where my brother still slept and my mum sulked. He lit a cigarette. I got out too but didn't know how to help. Memories of that earlier denied camping trip came rushing back to me, most painfully, as though the wrong had not been righted after all. I suspected I'd need another camping trip to wipe out the memory of this one as well as the one I'd missed. The thought exhausted me. I noticed that the boot of our car was open and so I went back for the suitcase. I wanted to do something but I wanted it to be something separate from the rest of my family. I lifted it out in such a way that it fell heavily down onto the grass at my feet. From inside the car, my mum snapped at me. Claire's mum looked at the case and smiled. It was wrong to bring this kind of luggage camping, her smile said. I lifted the case back inside the boot and fell into a heavy funk, both angry and disappointed with myself for showing how things really were with us.

It was completely dark by the time both tents went up. We said goodnight. So far, nobody had mentioned the overtaking on the road. Our tent was more like a gazebo. It was an older version of the more compact, modern one that Claire and her family had bought that summer, lending us their earlier incarnation for the weekend. The gazebo had giant PVC windows and was covered in a muddy yellow stripe and a big psychedelic flower print. Even in the dark, I knew it was the only one of its kind on the campsite. There was nothing to match it in stature or flair. Camping for us was something started in the past.

It was raining heavily now. My mum eventually agreed to leave the car, carrying my sleeping brother in her arms. I envied him his youth. He had no idea that this was a terrible family to belong to. Once we four were inside the gazebo, she asked my dad to go back outside. We'd forgotten the suitcase. I didn't offer to help this time. Inside, the tent smelt like plastic that wasn't unlike the fumes that came off my old Wendy house when it had been left outside in the midday sun. While Dad was gone, my mum placed my brother down inside the travel cot where he remained snug for the rest of the night, comfortably raised off the cold ground. We three slept in a compartment on a series of sun loungers and the contents of the airing cupboard from home. My mother had even brought the blankets from the bottom of the cupboard; the ones that usually lined the shelves. Everything felt damp.

I lay awake. I was waiting for my mum to break into her familiar snore. At home, the depth and timbre of it had driven my parents to separate beds early in their marriage. Our house had always been impossibly loud at night. It's one of the things I miss most about her; how she kept us all awake for years. Inside the gazebo, my parents had rowed again before bedtime, and loudly. The row was about the journey we had already taken. In particular, about the unexpected part of the road in which we had gone it alone. They argued for a good thirty minutes before realising, as they always did, that like most of their arguments it was built on a mutual irritation born of each other's personalities, rather than an attempt to solve a particular problem. This row seemed to tire my mum and so it didn't take long for her to fall asleep afterwards.

My dad and I let her snore on but didn't sleep ourselves. On the other side of Mum, I heard him twist and turn relentlessly. After what I imagined was some soul searching on his part on whether it was morally the right thing to do, he rose abruptly and told me he was going to sit in the car. I didn't see him again until the morning.

I waited until I heard the car door shut behind him

through the wall of the tent before I was able to relax myself. Everything was quiet now. I was able to enjoy that silence beyond the sounds coming from my dear mother. I listened to the rain and allowed myself to wonder if this is what it had been like on the Brownie Guide trip. On the campsite, with its flimsy streets, everything felt much closer at night.

You could hear people coughing only metres away. It was clear to me then that everyone had heard my parents rowing. Once they'd zipped up the tent door, they'd thought themselves secure. It occurred to me I might say something else out loud, to set myself apart from them. To let people know there were other types of people inside the tent with giant flowers on its side.

'We're not all like that,' I whispered, knowing only I'd hear it.

Beside me, my mum's snoring had risen to new heights. I turned from her and lay on my back with my arms crossed over my chest. I might lie like this when I die, I thought. In the distance, beyond the rain, I heard what I thought must be the sea crashing against the beach below the campsite. I closed my eyes and thought of the long draw of the waves and imagined myself there, free for a moment, charging through the surf. I wondered how much space, how much time I might need to live through in order to get to a fresh moment like that one out there.

We were up before the morning. There wasn't even

time to pack up the tent. My dad had spent the night in the car behind the steering wheel he told me, although he knew I already knew this. He had negotiated the leaving of the tent with the other dad. He had to get back. The plan had always been to stay two nights but I understood, looking into his eyes, that in the next five minutes he might disintegrate if it wasn't now. Things are easier to take apart than put together, so I helped my mum stow the travel cot back inside the car. The baby, fresh-faced and gargling like a happy brook, went in next. My dad took the suitcase in-hand. We said goodbye to Claire and her parents. Her dad understood, he said, although he looked like he didn't. Her mum was still smiling serenely at us and I could tell that mine didn't like that. I was exhausted, but more for what I hadn't experienced, then for what I had. Claire and I promised to see each other when she returned. All good things arrive first, I thought.

As our car sped away from the campsite, I peered out of the rear-view mirror to see if I had been right about the sea. I was disappointed to discover it was mainly land behind the campsite, but then, where a pair of fields dipped into a clear V, I caught a fleeting wink of blue, before the car abruptly dived inland.

Sayyida Nanda

Katherine Blessan

AN IMPISH GUST of wind swirled the dust in eddies around the yard before drifting down around Sayyida's feet. Sayyida lifted her head and gazed at the leaves dancing overhead, hearing the tinkly laughter of tiny fairies fluttering above her. She shifted the dust grits in her mouth and licked her lips in a vain attempt to remove the dust from her tongue.

'Quit your daydreaming, young lady!' A cracked voice called out, splitting the atmosphere and jerking Sayyida into action. She had only stopped her work for a minute or two to look up at the trees, but Aunty didn't miss a trick. She lifted the broomstick and began sweeping it back and forth, back and forth, moving the ever-increasing dust into piles. Once again, a gust of wind swept in and the piles of dust dispersed like children being set free at the end of the school day. Aunty Jaswinder bustled out of the house in a flurry of sari and jingling gold bangles and gave Sayyida's cheek a resounding slap.

Her face stung with the double effect of clinking metal and unforgiving palm.

'That's for your hopeless work. If you can't improve your work in the next half an hour, you'll be on your knees scrubbing the floor until I can see my face shine in it. Don't expect to eat your lunch until you're finished.'

OF COURSE, THE more Sayyida swept dust into piles in the yard, the more the wind whipped the dust up and around. Her arms ached with the thankless effort. Thirty minutes later, she felt a sharp yank on her ears.

'No good. Inside,' was all Aunty said before handing her a heavy brush and a bucket of water and pulling her inside the hut.

'What do I want to waste my time with you here for? I could be living the good life in Lahore if it weren't for you....' Jaswinder complained as Sayyida squatted down to scrub and scrub and scrub the stone floor: in one corner, around the next corner, in a circular motion here, backwards and forwards there. A sharp pain extended from one shoulder to the other and spiked down her spine. She gritted her teeth and blocked out the buzzing of Aunty's repeated grumbles. Her stomach was twisted with hunger, but it was 3 o'clock before Aunty granted her the freedom to sit down and handed her a bowl of rice, some dal curry and a chapatti. Too tired to talk, she scooped up the food with her hands as quickly as she could without giving herself indigestion.

SAYYIDA LOST TRACK of time, and followed the passage of the days between sunrise and sunset by daydreaming and counting the number of slaps she received. If she got less than three slaps, it was a good day. Aunty Jaswinder told her that she had been in Pakistan for three years now.

In good time, life was going to become 'better' for her, as she was to be married to Bopha, Aunty's oldest son. It didn't seem to matter that she was only ten and Bopha was twenty-two years old. He worked as a bus driver, ferrying teaming busloads of girls and boys to school from the villages to the nearby town and back again. Sayyida didn't have much to do with Bopha as he didn't talk to her, just grunted at her and withdrew to the back room when he came in most days. But recently, he had taken to looking at her in a way that made her shiver. She knew what marriage was, as her parents had been married in England before Dad slipped away onto the passing train that took him in the direction of the Land of Oz. That's what she told herself, anyway. But she didn't really know what marriage would involve. No one had told her anything. Even at school back in England, there had only been hints and silly talk from the naughty popular girls, but nothing concrete. All Sayyida knew was that she was too young to be getting married. Her parents and all her friends' parents had been a lot older than she was now. Her head ached with the puzzle of trying to work it all out. All Aunty Jaswinder would say was, 'You'll get used to it,' and Sayyida didn't ask her any more, scared of receiving further slaps.

Aunty had started calling her the 'mouse' as she was so quiet now. The only talking she did was in her head and the only words she used were the ones she whispered to her little friends, who lived inside her head, up in the trees or under her bed.

***

'DADDY'S LITTLE PRINCESS,' he used to call her. Sayyida was only five years old when he got on that passing train, but she remembered like it was in technicolour how he was in their towering terraced house. He used to sit her on his lap and tickle her cheeks with his whiskers and she'd giggle and wriggle until Mummy would tell him to stop. Sayyida would ask, 'Why should he stop?' and Mummy would look at her sternly, tap the tip of her nose and say,

'In case the laughter makes all your insides pop out.'

That just made her laugh even more.

AFTER HE GOT on that train, all the giggles stopped.

Daddy was the one who had lit all the fires and ignited all the happiness in their lives, or so it had seemed to Sayyida. Uncle Amir and his new wife moved into their house with his three children. Her cousins were very different living in her home than they had been when they met up at family celebrations and festivals. Samira pulled Sayyida's hair and pinched her whenever she wanted to play with her toys, and Zubeir sat in her chair, gave her snide looks and told tales on her, just because he could. She felt the baby was the only one who liked her, but maybe only because she couldn't speak yet. Uncle Amir did things to Sayyida and her sister, Munira, that she couldn't tell anyone about. She still cried now when she thought about it, though she tried not to think about it as she didn't want Aunty Jaswinder to hear her weep.

One afternoon, when Sayyida had just turned seven, Uncle Amir collected her from school. He picked her up in his dark blue spaceship car. Usually, the girls walked home from school as they lived close by, so when she saw the car she was surprised.

'Where's Munira?' she asked, as Uncle opened the backseat door of the spaceship and slid inside. He didn't say anything until he'd got in, closed the door and put on his seatbelt.

'Munira has stayed behind at school for a drama club.'

Munira had told Sayyida nothing about that, and normally she told her everything. Munira knew how much she liked drama. A little stab of jealousy pricked her heart. Rain began to splash against the windows of the spaceship and Sayyida heard the swoosh, swoosh, swoosh of cars and trucks rushing past on the motorway. She realised that they weren't going home.

'Where are we going?' she asked.

'We're going on holiday,' Uncle said.

'But I don't have any of my things with me!'

'Oh, don't worry about that,' he said, laughing. 'There's a suitcase in the boot of the car for you with all you will need for your holiday. What a nice surprise, hey!'

'What about Mummy and Munira? I want them to come with me.' Sayyida didn't like this plan half as much as he expected her to. Watching the flick, flick, flick of the windscreen wipers, she moved her index fingers back and forth, mimicking. Uncle Amir passed her a bag of her favourite lemon sherbets. She popped one in her mouth and crunched straight down on the middle, releasing the sharp tingle of sweetness and waited for his response.

'This is a special holiday just for you. Your mum is going to stay back to look after the rest of the kids, and Munira is going to stay at school. You'll be having fun while she stays in Bradford.'

'Where are we going?'

'To see all your aunties and uncles. They've got a special welcome party for you when you arrive.' It sounded nice but she didn't want to go alone without

Mummy and Munira so she sat in the back of the car, and looked out of the window at the rain-slashed roads, her stomach churning. It was no good saying how she felt to Uncle Amir as he would just laugh and tell her how ungrateful she was being.

THERE WAS NO celebration party when Sayyida got off the plane; the only friendly greeting was the sign on the road from the airport saying 'Welcome to Pakistan.' Uncle Amir passed her into the hands of a sweaty driver who took her through the big city, past the blaring of horns, higgledy-piggledy traffic and the intermittent smells of spices and incense out on the potholed and dusty roads to the village where Aunty Jaswinder and Bopha lived.

SHE NEVER SAW him again.

'SHE'S A BIT smaller than I was expecting,' Aunty Jaswinder grumbled to her neighbours. 'I thought she'd be big and fat, coming from England.' She said nothing to Sayyida then. But the next day she had plenty to say, shouting orders at her. Aunty got her working: dusting and sweeping; washing and drying clothes. There was no washing machine, so washing clothes was hard and backbreaking. She had never known such squalor before. Inside she was screaming, 'Get me out of here! I want to go home!' Even though things hadn't been the same after Daddy went on his train, at least life was better there than here, and at least she had Mummy and Munira. Sayyida didn't scream aloud though as there was no point. Aunty Jaswinder held her with a hooked claw and she knew that there was no getting out unless and until Mummy came to take her home. She would come, wouldn't she?

***

A FEW MONTHS before her eleventh birthday, Sayyida noticed the trickle of blood oozing down her legs and ran to the outside toilet to see what was happening. She was terrified. She was bleeding from inside and had no idea why. She stuffed a handful of cleaning cloths in her knickers, then went to Aunty Jaswinder to tell her what was happening, as she had no one else to tell.

Aunty's response was unexpected. She snorted and said, 'No need to worry. It's normal. You're becoming a woman. It's early, but the bleeding has been known to start in girls as young as nine. It'll soon be time to give you to my son.' That was it, end of conversation. Sayyida was told nothing about why her periods were starting. Aunty gave her a pile of thick sanitary pads and told her to use them when she was bleeding, the only item that

Aunty ever gave her for her own personal use.

AFTER THIS, EVENTS speeded up and Sayyida soon found that she was the centre of attention in a way that she'd not experienced before. Life lifted off its hood and revealed a bewildering kindness to her. Cousins and other aunties and uncles came to visit and she found herself being kissed on the cheeks and hugged many times as though she were the guest of honour and not the slave that she had been for so long. A local Iman came to the home, and Sayyida sat on the floor next to Bopha whilst he prayed over them and proclaimed the best day for the wedding as being in twenty days' time. The following day was the Mayun ceremony where two of Aunty's nieces, sweet, friendly girls called Amina and Waseema, both in their mid-teens, covered Sayyida's face, arms and feet in a yellow paste called 'uptan' to beautify her in preparation for marriage. For the first time in a long time, Sayyida was giggling as the paste almost went inside her eyes and mouth a couple of times.

'Does it taste good?' Amina laughed as Sayyida worked hard with her tongue to avoid swallowing a globule of uptan that had dribbled into the corner of her mouth.

This ceremony conferred on Sayyida the honour of not doing any housework until the wedding, and Bopha moved out of the hut to stay with some neighbours until the wedding day. The excitement was building up around Sayyida, and she felt as though maybe this marriage was going to be something good after all, and she hushed her fears and the sharp pang of her mother not being around. For the first time ever, Aunty Jaswinder nodded and bobbed around her, serving her sweet meats and treating her kindly, though she avoided looking Sayyida in the eyes whilst doing this. Sayyida barely knew what to do with herself, never having a moment to call her own until this time, but the other girls talked and played with her and she was content.

SAYYIDA WALKED INTO the hut one day after playing with the girls in the yard and overheard Jaswinder talking to one of the other aunties in the kitchen.

'The bride price has already been paid by Sayyida's English family. The money they paid covered all the wedding expenses.'

Sayyida moved out of earshot after this point, but her heart stung with the knowledge that her family had been complicit in this. Did 'her English family' mean that her mother supported this marriage, or was it all Uncle Amir's doing?

The doubt about her mother gnawed away at her happiness in the days to come, in spite of the singing, the dancing, the drumming, and the general celebratory atmosphere. One night, Sayyida sat up in a tangled mess of sheets after a vivid dream. Her mother's voice had hissed at her, 'Sayyida, Sayyida; you're nothing. You never have been. Why do you think I sent you away?'

BY THE TIME the actual wedding day came, all Sayyida could feel was a dull buzz through her senses. Her hands having been painted in henna and her arms covered in jangling gold bracelets, she sat quivering underneath the beautiful gown and veil that was covering her body. Bopha sat shyly next to her. Before she knew what was happening, the Iman had prayed for them, a sugary pudding was popped into her mouth from Bopha's palm, and everyone was laughing and clapping while two fairies danced in a circle above her head.

AS SWIFTLY AS the relatives had come they were gone again, and Sayyida was left with Bopha, alone for the first time. His physical urgency terrified her and left her bruised and shaking. Over the next few days, Sayyida came to realise how demanding marriage could be. She had been so caught up in a whirl of festivities that she had not thought about what the reality might be and she had no mother to warn her. Bopha was not deliberately unkind, but she felt his pressure on her like a tiger pouncing on a rabbit, and he still did not speak to her so she had no cushioning of gentle words from the harsh truth.

With the relatives gone, life was back to normal for Sayyida. The hitting and the cursing from Aunty Jaswinder resumed, almost as if she felt threatened by Sayyida's marriage to her son. Sayyida retreated into silence once more and her fairies hid high up in the tree where she couldn't see them. This time it was more difficult as she had experienced the fullness of life here and knew what it could be like. One night as she lay sleeping, tense in the bed next to Bopha, her mind was filled with dreams. She saw herself as an adult woman walking up some steep stairs. At the top of the steps was a great oak door. She knocked on the door and it opened. A powerful light flooded in as the door opened and she was almost blinded, but it was a sweet light rather than one that pained or disturbed her. A warm, firm hand reached out and drew her through the door. She woke up gasping and sat bolt upright in bed. Although it was just a dream, it was so crisp and clear that its imprint stayed with her. This was more than her imaginary world of fairies and whispers and dancing. She had felt a tangible presence strumming on her heart strings with a melody that sang to her through the difficult times.

FIVE MONTHS LATER, there was a knock at the front door. Sayyida was sweeping near the window in the back room, her body contorted as she squeezed into the narrow space between the bed and the window.

'I'll get it!' Jaswinder called, and Sayyida heard the pad pad of bare feet moving towards the door. An official sounding male voice spoke.

'Is there a young girl called Sayyida Nanda residing in this house?' That surname had not been used since she was back in England. Sayyida echoed her almost forgotten name,

'Sayyida Nanda.'

For a minute all that could be heard was the ka ka of the crows and the buzzing of a fly that bounced dizzily off the walls in a frantic attempt to escape.

'Yes there is, sir.' Aunty's voice bowed and scraped, deferential to the core.

The strumming reached its highest pitch.

Relevant

Anna Orridge

MRS GILLIES STOOD up, one hand fiddling with the button of her cardigan, the other shelled over the whiteboard clicker. She waited for silence. I and all the other students shifted in our seats and exchanged nervous grins.

'This photograph of Mrs Pankhurst is iconic. Absolutely ICONIC.' Her voice trembled with reverence. Even her earlobes quivered.

She pressed the clicker and the image appeared on the screen.

When I thought of suffragettes, I always pictured women with sashes draped over broad shoulders, marching about with serious frowns and stately placards. But this was a tiny woman in an outsized hat, swept clean off her feet by PC Plod. He looked all upbeat and cheerful.

Nate, who was on the next table, snorted. 'Looks like he's taking out the rubbish.'

I felt guilty, but I was glad somebody else laughed. It *did* look funny. Mrs Pankhurst's mouth was open in the way my mum always said would guarantee you a lovely meal of flies. She was shouting something. 'Votes for Women!' Or maybe just telling the cop to let go.

Mrs Gillies fiddled with the beads connected to her specs. She ignored Nate. 'So class, an image of vulnerability as well as strength. Things seemed hopeless for the suffragettes at this point in time. But they still won. Why?'

Nate sucked his lips and raised a hand. 'People got fed up of all those marches and paintings getting cut up and hunger strikes. All those stunts, you know.'

Mrs Gillies tilted her head to one side. 'Stunts, you say? Innovative publicity I would call it. Personally, I think they succeeded because they were right. There's something about that quality of rightness that tends to prevail, whatever the circumstances. Anyway...' She cleared her throat. 'I would like you to take a leaf out of their book. You have social media, modern communications and online platforms. I want you to radically repurpose that image. Make it relevant to a modern audience. It can be for activism or even something commercial. You're going to work on it in groups of three.'

Her eyes alighted on me and she nodded. 'I expect great things from you, Ginny.'

I smiled weakly. Jeez. You make one puny little animated badge for the college website, and old people suddenly think you're Ginny Holder, Programmer Extraordinaire, Steve Jobs The Second. She pointed at Puneet and pinched her fingers together. 'I'd like you to pair up with Puneet and...' Before I had time to object, Nate had pushed his chair right up next to mine. '...Nate. Is that okay?' He gave me one of his stupid grins. Like we were sharing a joke, though we've hardly ever spoken. I nodded. What else could I do?

'Right. You've got the weekend to come up with your ideas. There is a prize, you'll be glad to know – tickets to Alton Towers. I won them in a competition at Christmas, but fairgrounds are not my cup of tea, so I'm more than happy to pass them on. Groups one and two will present next week, groups three and four the week after that.'

The suffragettes were not exactly *my* thing. Mum was always going on about how I had to vote when I was old enough, because better women than me had died so I could have the privilege. There's nothing like having gratitude rammed down your throat to make you feel exactly the opposite.

But, I *loved* theme park rides. Rollercoasters were the best. Nothing beats that catch in your throat just as the car is about to drop, all the little jolts and rattles, putting your head back and letting the air whip round your fingers. Sure – whip? lash? – either's fine with me.

That was worth making an effort for.

***

'SO, WE'D LIKE to introduce you to…the Suffrage Diet!' Nadia stepped back from the whiteboard with a royal flourish of the hand.

A few titters bounced around the class.

The website was up on the screen, the Mrs Pankhurst photograph right at the top. 'Three weeks on our hunger strike and you'll be light enough to lift like this lady.'

Mrs Gillies blinked a few times and crossed her arms. 'Well, that's certainly a radical repurposing.'

THE NEXT GROUP did a prototype for a backpack, with a little muppet-style Mrs Pankhurst as the sack, and long chains for the straps, with handcuffs at the end. Apparently, she'd shout "Universal Suffrage" when you pressed her tummy.

I thought that was quite good. Mrs Gillies didn't, though. Especially when they showed how you could zip Mrs Pankhurst's mouth up. Mrs Gillies' eyebrows came together like two knitting needles and she pursed her lips. 'That puts the ironic into iconic.'

SO, ALL TO play for.

NATE, PUNEET AND I hadn't come up with an idea yet, but we had to do our presentation on Monday. We went to the college cafe after class to discuss it.

Puneet twirled her pencil and chewed the unicorn rubber at the end of it. Seventeen years old and she's got a unicorn pencil? I swallowed my scorn down with my coffee. Nate slumped back, playing with the cords of his hoodie. He winked at me.

A lot of girls in our year thought Nate was good looking. Sure, he had stormy grey eyes, broad shoulders and dimples, but he also had this sort of half-arsed mohican thing going on, hair sticking up in the middle in silly little tufts. It always made me think of a stegosaurus. He kept trying to barge into my conversations with other people. But he was never quite aggressive enough to make me feel it was okay to tell him to piss off.

Puneet suddenly lifted her pencil in victory. 'I've got it! How about a dance routine?'

I choked a bit on my coffee, cupping a hand over my mouth. 'Yeah. Right. We'll call it the suffratwerk.'

Nate breathed in deeply. 'Sounds good to me.'

Puneet threw a strand of her hair back. 'Just hear me out.'

She pulled Nate up by the hand and drew his arms round the front of her waist. 'It could be like a music video. You know, the guy lifts the girl up from behind, rock 'n' roll style. It might go viral.'

I shook my head. Seeing Puneet and Nate side by side made me think, though. He was tall, probably the tallest guy in our year, and Puneet looked tiny next to him. Her big eyes and the cute messy bun she wore her hair in had earned her the nickname Tinkerbell.

Puneet coughed. 'So…what do you think?'

I looked down at the photograph, then back up at them again. 'Yeah, no. I don't think the dance thing would work. Mrs Gillies doesn't like comedy stuff, does she? But how about this…?'

***

WE WERE GETTING a lot more attention than I had anticipated. Eight o'clock Saturday night on a high street with a load of pubs probably wasn't the best location for filming.

'Kissagram?' a girl shouted at Nate. He gave her a twirl and tipped his stupid plastic policeman helmet at her.

We were going to make a gif – Nate lifting Puneet off the floor. I hadn't worked out the caption yet. I needed something short and snappy. Uplifted? Lift your voices? No doubt, shout out…Christ, that sounded like a cheerleading chorus.

'Look, can we get this done?' I muttered, fiddling with my phone. 'We don't want you getting arrested for impersonating a policeman, do we?'

In all honesty, there was little chance anyone would mistake Nate for a real PC. Not with that helmet we'd bought from Poundland.

Puneet, on the other hand, was looking pretty natty. I'd got her decked out in my mum's old gypsy skirt and ankle boots. Once I'd got the black-and-white filter on, she'd make a quite decent Mrs Pankhurst.

'Okay,' I called. 'Ready?'

Nate nodded and wrapped an arm round Puneet's waist. He hoisted her up a few inches. The big black hat fell over her eyes. She began to buck her head like a horse's to knock it back into place.

I rolled my eyes.

'Okay, okay…' Puneet raised her hand. 'Sorry.'

I zoomed in.

Nate squeezed her again. Then he did some Elvis-style thrusting behind her, his eyes on me all the time. He even stuck his tongue out slightly.

'Hey,' I shouted. 'That's disgusting.'

Puneet arched her head away from his. 'It's okay, Ginny. He's just messing around.' But her smile was strained. She tugged her tunic down over her leggings.

I pressed Pause. 'Right,' I snapped. 'Are we just taking the piss or are we going to make this gif?'

'Sorry, sorry.' Nate raised his palms. 'Honestly, Ginny. We'll do it properly.'

'One more chance. I'll count you in,' I muttered.

'Three…Two…One.'

And Record.

Nate kept his eyes on the camera. A smirk made his dimples a little deeper. He lifted Puneet up and started walking forwards. But his arm was a lot further up this time, right under her breasts. Puneet's eyes widened. 'LET ME GO!' But he just pressed harder.

I had a flashback to this one time when my dad was squeezing air out of an inflatable mattress at a campsite. He'd folded it over and gritted his teeth as he squeezed it. Just like Nate was doing to Puneet now. I felt sick.

'Fucking put her down. NOW!' I shouted.

He actually tightened his grip, but then Puneet brought her jaws down on his bicep and bit hard. He yelped in shock. She brought her head back and hit him hard in the chest.

'Ooof.' He dropped her.

She staggered to one side.

'Little bitch…' he muttered, examining the bite mark.

Puneet ran over to me. Tears sent long trails of mascara down her cheeks.

I grabbed her wrist. 'Are you okay?'

She didn't answer, but buried her head in my shoulder.

'What the hell? What's wrong with you?' I shouted at Nate, waving my phone.

He flapped a hand at us, 'Come off it. She was asking

for it. And so are you, staring at me all the time.' With that, he walked off.

'That was amazing,' I said, stroking Puneet's back as she sniffed.

She raised her head, wiping her eyes with her sleeves. 'What was amazing?'

'Your moves. That kung fu shit.'

'I did a self-defence class once. I guess it must have stuck.' She tapped the top of her head, her cute bun all picked loose.

I looked down at the paused video. The still on the screen was a disturbingly good copy of the original photograph.

***

NATE DIDN'T DO the presentation with us. He was in class, though, hands on the back of his head, with its stupid Not Mohican and its red stripes.

Puneet and I came up to the front. I stuck the memory stick into the laptop.

'You sure about this?' I mouthed at Puneet. She nodded, eyelashes lowered.

'So,' I coughed. 'Our idea was to take the photograph and make it into a short film. A demonstration of self-defence.'

Mrs Gillies sat up with interest and tipped her spectacles down her nose.

I pressed Play. The film started just as Nate was lifting Puneet off the floor.

PUT THE RUBBISH OUT flashed at the bottom of the screen as he lifted her off the floor.

When he squeezed Puneet, the 'SH' at the end of RUBBISH bumped into the next word to make SHOUT.

The letters around it rapidly rearranged themselves to make the words BITE, then BUTT, as Puneet clamped her jaws down on his arm and whacked the back of her head into him. A few other students gasped and winced.

The last letters were left on the screen. They came together to make the word OUT, then faded as Puneet staggered away from Nate. A little rubber on the screen rubbed the whole of him out, from the top to bottom.

That had taken me ages to do on my PC. But all the effort was worth it when I saw his reaction. The dimples had gone. Fury contracted his brows.

'Wow,' someone said with a low whistle. 'Way to go, Tinkerbell.'

Puneet beamed.

I coughed. 'And can we just have a round of applause for Nate and his acting? I mean, he REALLY looks shocked in the video, don't you think?'

Everyone clapped. I kept my eyes on Nate. He tilted his head back and blinked. He wanted me to think he wasn't bothered. Fact was, though, he couldn't meet my eyes.

Mrs Gillies tipped her specs at us both and smacked her hands on the desk. 'Ingenious, girls. I think that's a terrific way to make that image relevant.'

I smiled and nodded.

I wanted to tell her that "Relevant" didn't have to be giffed up and filtered and animated to make sense to us.

Relevant could be grainy black and white in ankle boots and an old-style hat.

Relevant could have the gramophone crackle and static of over a century of change. We'd still hear it.

After all, gramophones are pretty damned cool.

***

PUNEET AND I leaned back into our seats as the roller-coaster restraints came down over our heads.

'Oh my God. I'm going to die. Kill me now,' she shrieked, shaking her head as the car began to climb the first slope. She screwed her eyes shut and cackled manically, knocking the backs of her sandals against the seat.

Obviously, Nate was not invited on our winner's day out to Alton Towers.

I must admit, I used to look down on Puneet before this whole suffragette video thing. I took all that girly stuff and squealing at face value. My bad. She isn't stupid at all.

We were nearly at the top. I loved the way the car just

kept creeping, creeping upwards. My stomach lurched as it tipped forwards.

I took Puneet's hand and she squeezed my fingers. That brief, agonised moment of stillness. I could only see the thinnest slash of track beneath us. Together, we were ready to drop.

Those Who Trespass Against Us

Julie Bull

MY DAD IS always on at me to murder him *when the time comes*. Though he is a bit vague about when this time will be.

'Once I don't know where I am, then I'm counting on you to put me out of my misery, Lucy. I am not to be left in agony like some animal.'

I could tell him not to be silly, or say that he is in fine fettle, but it would be a lie. So I don't bother. It's been three years since the diagnosis. The last round of chemo has failed to halt the progress of his cancer and he is getting weaker. No further treatment is on offer. So we are somewhere near the end and there is no one to care for him. Only me.

I've had to put up with his carry on all morning to get him ready for church. First, he downright refused to get out of his bed and since then he's been shouting and flailing and calling me all the names under the sun. Now, finally, he's straightened out and ready – wearing his checked brown suit and a burgundy silk tie – the same one he wore to my wedding all those years ago. Almost human, he looks.

'Have we time for a whisky, Lucy?'

He looks at me with these cloudy, pleading eyes and I want to say to him that I remember. I remember everything. Instead I tell him he'll have whisky back at the house soon enough. I part the curtains and it's a relief to see the taxi still waiting in the drizzle.

My daughter's first Holy Communion is a big deal. It's all about our standing both in the community and in the eyes of the church. I know I have to care about this despite being lapsed. It means a lot to everyone, to our Anna in particular. So I do care. I won't let her down.

Months ago, Paul put the laptop screen in front of my face to show me a YouTube clip of some American family who had recorded every moment of their daughter making her first holy communion.

'You want to go for something like this.' Those were his instructions.

This video shows 'Mom', who has set out an all-white buffet in the massive kitchen in one of those houses that all American families live in, if you believe the telly version of America. On the large table, about fifty helium balloons are hovering over crucifix shortbreads, marshmallow biscuits, and a tall, sparkly cake. The family—there are loads of them and they are all smiling—come into the kitchen one by one and the mother stands by as though it has been no effort at all to have created this spread. Her hair is bouffant and her smile as white as the buffet. The family bob around each other like a big happy gang. White is fitting, Paul says, because it is the colour of purity.

We went for a lace dress in the end, a flower garland and silk drawstring bag, silk ballet pumps and plain white tights. I don't approve of tiaras and make-up, though both are getting to be a bit of a trend. There's families round our way without a brass penny that will bankrupt themselves to splash out on communion dresses and all of the razzmatazz that goes with it, even though our church has openly said it's not really what it's supposed to be about. So I know Father Michael also doesn't agree with tiaras and frills and certainly not covering kiddies' faces in make-up. I like Father Michael – he always looks at me like I matter when I go up to refuse the sacrament at weddings and christenings, folding my arms over my chest to signal that I want to take a blessing only.

Maybe he's disappointed but he wants me to know that the Lord loves me anyway, which is a nice idea, even if I don't believe a word of it. I often wonder what Paul tells Father in the confession box. Whether the sins he commits are mortal or venial. I know that at each confession the slate is wiped clean, which is dead handy.

For the last seven days, I have pushed a rolling pin across biscuit dough and pulled white icing into the shape it needs to be to cover my crap baking. I have sifted flour and pounded and rolled dough and paste. Now I've even managed to get the old sod to the church in one piece and for all that I think I deserve a bloody medal, not that I'll get a word of thanks from my other half.

We pull up to St Mary of Magdalene and Paul's face looms down through the car window, pointing at his watch to tell us we are late. His face is round and red, his chin nicked from shaving. You can see the anger seething beneath his skin.

'You're the last to arrive for fuck's sake. I thought you weren't coming.'

'We're here now.' I announce the obvious. Anything to calm him down.

By some miracle the sun has come out and is shining through the horse-chestnut trees outside St Mary's. I watch Anna flitting among her friends. They're sort of skittering and twirling about and they all look like tiny brides, which gives me the heebee jeebies. Eventually she rejoins us for a photo. Her granddad places his big bony hand around her waist and manages a smile through the dentures that he's never got used to. It is time to go in and receive the Eucharist.

This is the church where Paul and I were married,

thirteen years ago. As we take our place in the pew, I remember that day. It was a long walk down the aisle; every step such an effort to take, like I was wading through oil to get to him. Paul left it very late to turn round and face me and when he did I just thought, who is this guy? It sounds weird I know, but it was as if he was a total stranger. But I was going to marry him anyway. I was happy to be given away if it meant I could get away from my dad and be part of something else.

Today, Father Michael raises his arms in welcome.

'Father we thank you for these your children. Children, God called you by your name at your baptism and now the way to full Communion lies before you. Set your feet firmly onto that path and learn to trust Jesus always.'

The congregation begins the call and response. Then it's the Lord's Prayer and I join in because I remember all the words from school.

Give us this day our daily bread, deliver us from evil, forgive those who trespass against us.

I was nine years old when my mum had two strokes in the space of a few months and then died. It breaks my heart when I think of it because I feel so sorry for the little girl I was then. I don't honestly know if I miss her but I wish she'd stayed around. After that, my dad brought me up. Did the best he could, putting aside his own grief to do it. Well, that's one version of the story anyway.

'A man has needs.' Was what my grandmother would say, in a voice hinting at things I couldn't be expected to understand.

The fact that my poor father's needs remained unmet was offered by way of explanation for his foul temper. His moods got darker as each of my birthdays passed. By the time I was fourteen, he had a certain look in his eye that followed me across the room and made me put the chair against my bedroom door every night. As if that could stop him.

I left home when I was seventeen. Ran away to Manchester where I got a job in a hotel and rented a room in a house down by the canal, not realising that I was moving into the area where all the gays lived. It didn't bother me; I actually loved the fact that no men ever looked at me there. Out of some sense of duty, I still visited my dad most Sundays. I would fetch him some shopping and make a hot meal, do a bit of cleaning and always as I gathered my things to leave, he would kick off – telling me I'd been sleeping with all kinds of men and calling me a bitch to leave him. And then the shouting would turn to tears and pleading for me to come home.

'I need you Lucy, I can't be living here alone an old man.'

Just before my twenty-fourth birthday, I bought a part-share in a flat in the centre of Manchester on a special scheme for first time buyers. It had a balcony large enough for me to set out a small table and chairs; hang some outdoor lights. It looked like something from a magazine. Every evening when I caught a glimpse of those chairs on the balcony, I was absolutely made up. I had this sense that I had made something good out of nothing much.

By the time I met Paul, I'd got myself a qualification in hospitality management and was a team leader in the hotel chain that first employed me. My sights were set higher and I'd even started to think about a degree. Paul was a regular at the Millennium Inn, so we often exchanged small talk and he began to invent all sorts of excuses to talk to me, slowly getting more jokey and flirty. He made a lot of the fact that we were both from Liverpool and shared the same scouse sense of humour. He wore sharp suits and well pressed shirts in colours that brought out the ice blue of his eyes. I liked how clean and smart he looked; and I laughed at his jokes, though they weren't that funny.

He took me out to dinner on one of my rare evenings off. It was early May and the weather was glorious; blossom all over the trees outside the town hall in Albert Square. We ate at one of the smart new restaurants that were beginning to open all over town. We drank cocktails with salt round the rim of the glass. My head was swimming by the time I invited him back to sit on my balcony. We drank wine looking out over the chimneys and cranes beyond.

'You are just what I have been looking for,' he said, like I was the perfect outfit, or something thing on a menu. Then he unwrapped me from my clothing and had sex with me like I wasn't really there. After that it was as though I'd signed on some invisible dotted line, like he owned me. He stayed at my flat whenever he was in town. He left shoes in my narrow hallway and shaving gear in my tiny bathroom. He took charge of things for me; fixing broken taps and getting quotes for insurance. It was a relief after so long on my own. I turned the feeling of being looked after at last, into a love story.

Paul worked in IT and was dead ambitious, just like me. He said we made a great team. He also said he admired my independence, which is strange because what he did was set about destroying it. Over the next two years the value of my flat went up a lot and he persuaded me that selling it to put a deposit down on our new-build back in Liverpool would be the making of us. I would be back home with family to help us with the kids we hadn't yet had. Back where I belonged. Back to square one more like. I fought for my freedom only to give it up for a starter home in a cul-de-sac. To this day I don't really know why. I think I believed it might be my only shot at a proper family.

Anna is now in a long line of girls and boys who are

approaching the altar to take communion. I watch her as she makes her way towards the front. She's luminous, her grey blue eyes shining, her hands held in a prayer position and her expression as pious as can be. As she nears the front of the line, she cups her hands to receive the communion wafer and put it to her mouth. It is in her now, the body of Christ.

I know that I have been a disappointment as a wife and not only because I've turned my back on the church, though Paul puts all our misfortune down to this one fact. If I'd truly given myself to the Holy Mother church I would not have lost two babies before they were even born; and he would not hate me for it. His mother doesn't hold back. She thinks I'm a jinx on her precious son. 'You'll have no luck,' she told me, after Anna's baptism when I wouldn't take communion. There have been times when I've thought the old cow is right but then again, we have been given the gift of this one child. My girl – my Anna – I love the bones of her and I know that she'll forgive me for what I have to do. Until recently I had still hoped there was a chance of a brother or sister for her, which made it easier to bear when he climbed on top of me. Grunting his way to climax and sometimes calling me a whore. Just dirty talk – he says – no harm in it. I used to lie still afterwards, very still, wanting his sperm to settle inside me and give me one more chance. Now I want nothing of the sort. My future will be hard enough without another kid in tow.

THERE IS A party back at ours. Anna runs between friends and relatives, collecting her cards and presents. The biscuits I have slaved over are only crumbs now. I need to get Dad home and put him to bed. Paul is bladdered and I still don't have my license so it's another taxi and then the walk back for me. I don't mind because it's more time to think, more time away from Paul.

'You'll give your grand-da a special hug, so you will.' He lurches towards her, folding her into him and I see her curl her nose up.

'Goodbye, goodbye all,' he waves his arms at no one and I see Paul watching from the window.

He's obviously got a cob on. God knows why this time. I roll down the car window and feel the damp rush in. I'm not afraid of them anymore – not Paul, not Dad either. I don't know when it happened, but I feel brave. I feel like they owe me, the pair of them and I reckon that when the auld fellah is gone, the money from that house can get me out of here. I think of it all the time; I'll rent a place, somewhere further south – get a job, get a divorce, get a life. It's getting closer every day, the time when this will happen.

Back at Dad's, I turn up the thermostat and hear the boiler fire up. It's like winter has come on all of a sudden.

I put the kettle on to boil for his tea and then I help him up the stairs and into his pyjamas. I should wash him with a flannel like I usually do but it's late and I'm tired and I don't much care whether he is clean.

'It was a grand day, Lucy.'

'It was.' I say, plopping his dentures into a glass, lifting his legs up onto the bed and pulling the duvet up to his chin.

I pick up one of the two pillows next to his head. I close my eyes and feel the weight of it in both of my hands. I imagine him looking up, his eyes full of fear and I'm not even ashamed to say that this thought pleases me. But he's already drifting off to sleep and his eyes stay closed. I wonder if I'm strong enough to hold the pillow over his face if he puts up a fight. He's always been stronger than he looks. Eventually he will give in. In a single moment, he will let go, let me go.

I button up my trench coat and take my scarf from the peg in the hallway. As I open the door to leave, I hear him call – a cry which turns into a wail, intended to get me running back upstairs. I close the door behind me and walk out into the dark. Knowing that the time has very nearly come.

Past, Present, Future

Karen Hamilton

TIME PASSED IN changes of midwives and concerned faces. Blackness beckoned and the pain, so ceaseless, so overwhelming urged me to give into it with helpless gratitude. No last words of love, wisdom or regret, no care about the finality of death, just desire for the blessed escape that only it could offer.

I lived. My baby didn't. I blamed myself, I should've fought harder, been braver, done something, anything. Afterwards, a respect and fascination for mothers grew. I'd watch them, in awe of how outwardly unaffected they seemed by the experience. Naturally pre-occupied, they had babies to shower with attention, grateful for the gift of life. I focused my thoughts on women worldwide who gave birth without any care or support; I'd been fortunate not to be alone at my time of fear and loss; I was in a safe, clean place. I channelled my energy and grief to find ways to help those I could.

And now…

I am a mother; grateful, yet scarred by memories and the reality of keeping small humans alive and safe, loved, protected, nurtured, educated, warm, happy, healthy. All these importances …

Today, as I stand opposite my son – by law an adult yet still my child – I can't read his expression. I know this is deliberate, he has always been sensitive to moods, to situations, to others. It pains me that I can't protect him, that I've failed again and that I will lie to him and he to me. Real conversations are off-limits because we'd have to voice and give life to our fears.

'It will be alright,' I say.

Lie number one. Our lives are about to be ripped apart.

He still trusts me, that's the worst of it. His eyes, although undeniably older, look at me for guidance. I want to tell him that I wish we lived in a different world, one where fear, misunderstanding and intolerance didn't disintegrate into hate, forcing people to harm others they don't even know and a respect for life was paramount.

'I'll be fine,' he lies back. 'I don't want you to worry.'

I'm terrified. How do you choose the words for one of the last conversations you may ever have?

'James came back alright,' he says.

I smile. 'Yes, he did.'

No he didn't.

James lives in the next village. He is not alright. I've

been friends with his mother, Elizabeth, since we were at school and she tells me that 'he's not quite right.' It's an understatement. He's permanently dazed. He engages in conversations by answering questions as if he's pre-programmed. He was always skinny, but now, I can't think of the right words to describe his skeleton. Elizabeth says he calls out at night, his screams are much worse than when he was a toddler, but when she rushes to his room, he is still and eerily calm. Sometimes, she says, she wonders if she dreamed it, if it is *her* who screams, reliving the nightmare of sending her only child away. Her husband has gone. Her brother, gone. Her father, long gone.

I have John. I'm lucky. I know he suffers too, but has been taught to hide his pain, outrage and emotions. Outwardly, he, like so many, stays strong for me, tells me '*it will be alright.*' Even though we both know the only outcome of being 'alright' is for our son not to go, not to see or experience the horror.

'They' talk about the '*greater good*', a '*worse outcome,*' '*duty,*' '*no choice,*' and while I understand '*things are the way they are*' it doesn't mean that I have to accept it. I don't have to understand war and suffering; all the lost men and women. If I just gave up, I know John would understand. I'm sure he feels it too. Sometimes I think we should make a pact, go together, give in to the comforting pull of the blackness and oblivion, but we are luckier than lots.

I hug my child tightly the night before, fighting back my pain, my despair, my failure, my rage. I don't lie, I don't say it will be alright. I tell him I love him and I say my good-byes silently. I know I won't bring myself to say the words tomorrow. Instead, I've decided, I'll say 'good luck.' Maybe, just maybe, this time will be different, perhaps my change of words will make all the difference. I'm clutching the final slivers of hope because some of the last words I said to my eldest and middle sons were:

'Time will pass quickly.' 'I love you.' 'It will be alright.' And: 'Good-bye.'

Yet, it wasn't alright, time passed slowly and one Thursday afternoon, one Saturday morning and one Wednesday evening I discovered it really had been good-bye. I can remember the moments of blessed ignorance before each time I was informed that I'd lost another child.

However, when the moment comes, I do say 'Good-bye,' after I tell him how much I love him.

Because what else could I say?

Hope ebbs and flows. We are bombarded with *news*, bad and good. Horrific and uplifting. Women are encouraged to *have more babies*. Grace down the road would love a baby but hasn't been able to conceive. My cousin's daughter doesn't want children. I briefly foster twin boys who have been orphaned. I try not to get too attached but they are such a delightful distraction that I can't help it. When the time comes for me to say good-bye, I adopt two cats. I name them Hope and Patience.

Two hundred and twenty days later, my son comes home. He seems... 'alright', but weary and quiet. I don't ask questions.

I hold back tears of relief and gratitude, mixed with guilt for all those who are still suffering. But, tonight, I will allow myself a gift: Hope for the future and a dream of peace for all.

Tiny Valentines

Angela Readman

EVERYONE HAD LOST their minds and Rudolph Valentino was to blame.

It was August. The air was billowed with steam and vowels blunt as bread knives. I left the chemist's pondering the priests' socks. The cotton had faded and they'd sold out of black clothes dye. The shop bell jangled, and I heard someone whisper '*Rudolph Valentino*'. Two women were whispering. One lifted a hand to her mouth, the basket on her arm lilting, the strawberries inside falling into the street. Looking around the village, several women were pulling cotton handkerchiefs from up their sleeves. *Have you heard? It can't be true...It just can't be...*

Father O'Neill came around the corner and a girl rushed at him, grabbing his arm.

'Whatever's the matter, child?'

Poor Father, red as corned beef, fiddling with his collar didn't hold her back. She crumpled onto his chest sobbing. He patted her shoulder, uselessly.

'Now, now,' I said, unloading the girl into my arms. Florrie Millicent, that was her. Flirty lass, all lipstick and rat-a-tat shoes.

'Don't give me none of that heaven shite, Father. I *need* him *here*,' she said.

Her sobs vibrated through my breast bone. I looked down at her hat, her head on my chest like a drooping red tulip. It was the first time I spoke to Florrie Millicent, and the first time I'd held anyone in years.

THE PRIEST'S FINGER turned silver, running it over the inky paper the following day.

'Do *you* like the cinema?' he asked, 'this Valentino fellow?'

I served stew. 'Heavens, no. I've never understood what you *do* in there, just sat twiddling your thumbs in the dark.'

He nodded. The movie star was dead, but it didn't end there. Yesterday, a woman in Iceland drank her own tears laced with arsenic. Drop by drop, she caught them in a jar. Today, two American girls leapt off a rooftop, summer skirts flapping in the wind. The notes they'd left read: *I love you, Rudolph,* or some such malarkey. Madness.

'You don't think something like that could happen here?' Father asked, a finger wedged between chin and lip preventing a frown from falling on his face. I considered the women in my street: dragging in coal, wrestling wet sheets, scrubbing their doorsteps until their knuckles bled.

'People here have more sense,' I said.

I wasn't sure. Just last week, I'd found a magazine in church, spine cracked at a picture of Valentino, as if someone couldn't sit through the sermon without his face keeping them company. It lay beside a hymnal with *Mrs Valentino, Mrs F Valentino* scrawled inside the cover, over and over, like a schoolgirl practising who she intended to be.

I stamped the pepper on the table like a gavel and said, 'Don't worry, Father. It would never happen here.'

I SWEPT FALLEN leaves all September, chasing the footsteps of women wandering into church to light a candle. Florrie Millicent came often. She prayed and finally click-clacked into the confessional, face white as winter, eyebrows fine as a line of migrating birds. I polished the pews, listening.

'Bless me, Father, for I have...I'm pregnant...I didn't mean to. I mean, I've been out with lads from work, but I didn't... he put his hand on my.... but we didn't do *that*, Father, I swear. I know who the real father is, Father,' Florrie shuffled, 'It's Rudolph Valentino.'

She bolted out, bumping into me. I flapped my duster

like a yellow alibi. I wasn't that surprised by her confession. There was something about her. Flirting with anyone who paid her the slightest bit of attention. Often, she had a far-away look in church, words drifting over her, off in her own world. I was still soaking her lipstick off my blouse, so much blotting and dabbing for someone she'd never even met. I'd never understand.

***

I HADN'T CRIED at the funeral. I lit a candle afterwards and stared at the stone wall, darkened by smoke. It would have happened slowly, slow as my husband's chair developing a halo of dust off his hair. I pictured his chair, the stains of his work hands laid on the arms like silver gloves. Jesus, the church was filthy. I grabbed a coin and scraped wax off the table. Father O'Neill came in wearing a sweater, his breath was a ghost.

'So sorry for your loss, Elsie,' he said, 'terrible thing. How old was John?'

'Thirty-seven.'

Everything was about numbers now. Thirty-seven. Zero children. Third accident at the mill in two years. Wherever I went, I could see people calculate just how tragic it was – a sum of age and how many loved ones remained. One.

Father O'Neill watched me work without speaking. I wasn't sure he'd heard me. I speak too softly, everyone always said, except John, almost deaf from years at the mill.

'Most folks don't shape their words right,' he always said, 'they speak, but their lips barely move. Not you, so long as I can see you I always know what you're saying.'

My smile wasn't sure if it was the right shape or not – the smile of the loved.

Father O'Neill placed a hand on the table. I brushed flecks of wax into my palm. *Don't make me stop, Father. Please, don't make me go home...*

'Much better.' He stroked the smooth wood. 'You know, we could use someone like you around the place, Elsie. The pay isn't wonderful, but...'

I nodded, clenching a fist full of wax, unsure who 'we' was. I supposed he meant God.

***

THE CLOTHES-LINE OUTSIDE Florrie Millicent's had one skirt wedged between all the shirts like someone pushing in a queue. Walking home, I dipped underneath it, strung across the lane. Florrie lunged into the yard, the door slamming shut. She rattled the knob. The steely sound of a key clicked in the lock.

'Don't come back until you can talk sense!' her step-father yelled.

Mr Millicent sang beautifully at midnight mass. Glassy eyed, he'd sway to the music, carrying a tune surprisingly well. His voice was shredded by rage now. There was nobody around to calm him down. Florrie's mother passed when she was six, leaving her with a man who couldn't put in a straight pigtail, and two boys belonging to his late wife. The neighbours joked he probably wore both women out.

Florrie kicked the gate and glared over the wall. 'What you gawping at?'

It was clear she'd been crying. Her eyes looked raw and her eyebrows weren't pencilled on – leaving her face blank and impossibly young. I scurried along the lane.

The sky was charcoal, the last streaks of day smudging into dusk. Closing the curtains, I heard a knock, loud as a bailiff.

Florrie Millicent rubbed her arms. 'So, I hear you have a spare room?' she said, as if continuing a conversation, the conversation of me seeing her kicking a gate.

It wasn't a secret, what anyone had and didn't have. All our numbers are known. One surviving wife. No children. Two up. Two down.

'I sew in it,' I said, 'it's not *spare*.'

'I'll pay rent. I don't expect anything for nothing.'

I gripped the knob. Florrie wedged a stylish shoe in the door, 'I can't go home, just let me stay the night.'

'One night,' I said, 'that's your lot.'

I PRINTED *TENANT: Miss F Millicent* on the front of a rent book, after she'd stayed for three weeks. I wished I could add *(not friend)* and NO NONSENSE in bold, but of course, I couldn't. I wasn't sure what I could write.

The tenant is responsible for her own laundry.

The tenant will strip her own sheets.

The tenant is entitled to meals. She will wash her plate and cup.

The tenant won't sit in my husband's chair. She will hang up her coat.

The tenant will not say 'Come in, have at it' to a knock on the door when she's bathing.

The landlord requires access to the dining room to reach the toilet in the yard.

The tenant will cover up and stop trying to chat on such occasions. Bathing will not take an hour. No walking barefoot. No cracking toes. No borrowing hairpins. No leaving nail cuttings on the hearth. No abuse of the crossword.

The bible has Ten Commandments. So far, I had about fifty. I wanted her out.

Florrie sat by the fire, relaxed as a holidaymaker. Chewing a pen, she abandoned the crossword and doodled moustaches onto every face in the paper.

'You'll get chilblains sat like that.' I stared at her legs draped across the shape of my husband's fingers worn into the chair-arm. 'I was wondering what you'll do.' *Tell the father, buy a white dress, rush down the aisle and out of my life.*

'Do about what?' Florrie asked.

'Your position.' I glanced at her belly. The bomb of it.

'What position is that exactly?' Florrie giggled, relishing the comedy of my discomfort. I'd never admit I'd overheard, and she knew it.

'What have I told you about sweets?' I picked a liquorice wrapper off the rug and waggled it, rushing out.

The following Monday, I was blunter. It was a weekend filled with knickers on the clothes horse, cosmetics on the sink, and singing in the bath.

'Look,' I said, 'I know you're in trouble. Who's responsible?'

It was difficult to look at her. Late for work, pulling a chrysanthemum out of the vase and pinning it to her hat like nothing else mattered.

'You already know. Rudolph Valentino.' Florrie curled her bob into commas on her cheeks.

'Come on, you're in a situation. It's no time for daydreams.'

Florrie met my eye in the mirror and asked, 'When is the time to daydream, Elsie?'

My silence was an admission: I don't know. I never have.

I WANDERED BY the mill at lunchtime, wondering if I'd catch her sloping off with one of the lads, but I only saw Florrie on the steps, lighting a cigarette and staring at the clouds. I wanted to sit in my husband's chair, lay my hands where his were and let the quiet unfold around me, but my lodger was there. She wasn't in a hurry to go anywhere. I supposed she'd fallen out with some boyfriend and would leave when they kissed and made up. Perhaps I could speed up the process, once I discovered who he actually was.

Eventually, I followed her to the Saturday matinee. I crouched behind the war memorial opposite the cinema, hoping to spot her meet a lover, even a friend, who could take her off my hands. Florrie approached the ABC and turned sharply. One of her step-brothers was sitting on the steps. He hurried after her, grabbing her shoulder.

'Leave me alone!' She lurched free, flitted across the road and left him on the other side, a bus pulling up, blocking the crossing.

'What you doing here?' Florrie spotted me and yelled, her voice shaking.

'I was just shopping.' I lifted my basket as evidence.

Florrie peered inside. 'You came all this way for beeswax, when you can get it in the village? You're spying on me. Not just now, the other day at work. I waved, but you scurried off. What is it?' she asked, 'You think if you find me some *nice young man,* it will be the solution to everything? Is that it?' She sat on the war memorial steps, a cushion of paper poppies at her back. I sat beside her.

'It can't hurt, can it, to have a husband?'

'What if I don't want one? What if it wouldn't make me happy? If it would make no one happy.' People hurried by to the cinema. We sat still, a privacy drawn around us in the most public of places. 'If you *must* know who the men in my life are, alright, I'll tell you,' she said, 'There's Mr Brookes at the mill, who never docks my pay if I'm late. There's a lad at the factory who's my age, polite, and dull as toothache. There's Mr Taylor, the fishmonger, who gives me a lift home whenever I've watched the kids. That's about it. Take your pick, who would you rather I marry?'

I considered Mrs Brookes pushing her son's wheel-chair uphill. And Mrs Taylor, with her twin boys who bit her every chance they got.

'I like men,' Florrie said, 'I love their company, for a while. I've never saw one I'd want around all the time though, except Rudolph Valentino maybe.'

'That's just a daydream.'

'But it's my daydream and I love it.' Florrie opened the locket around her neck and gazed at a picture of the star like her personal tiny valentine.

MR MILLICENT STOOD outside my door waiting for us to

return. I left Florrie alone with her father and busied myself in the kitchen.

'You come to your senses yet?' he asked, 'You coming home?'

The kettle boiled. I couldn't hear the girl, only man and steam.

'There isn't a clean shirt in the house. The kitchen's a bombsite. Pack your stuff and come home. Your brother will marry you, if no one else will. We'll get something sorted. You're showing us up.'

I carried in the teapot and cups. Mr Millicent gripped Florrie's forearm.

'Maybe you can talk some sense into her,' he said, 'she can't just stay on her own with you. What will people think?'

I looked at Florrie hanging her head. I wondered what it was like growing up in that house. Endless shirts to iron, dinners to cook, dishes plonked on her lap when she was a child. Being a girl in that place took work. I set the pot down.

'You need to let go.' I lay my hand on Mr Millicent's fingers clamped to Florrie's arm. He looked down at my fingers on his. Together, we let go.

'Pack your shit, Florrie,' he said, 'I'm serious.'

Florrie remained silent. I heard her.

'Your daughter's welcome to stay for as long as she likes, Mr Millicent. Perhaps you could visit at a more convenient time.'

He didn't wait to be shown the door. He slammed it, rattling Jesus on the wall. The pot stewed, I poured tea. Florrie heaped sugar onto a soggy spoon, dripping lumps into the bowl.

'Well, if you're stopping,' I said, 'you'd better stop singing in the bath. You sound like a cat on laughing gas.'

THE VILLAGE WHISPERED when Florrie passed on the street. Spring was in the air and the girl's bump was plainer than day. She walked to work, brushing past dirty words, not letting them touch her, unashamed.

'That tenant of yours, has she admitted who her fancy fellow was?' the priest asked.

'Rudolph Valentino,' I said.

'Poor girl must be simple.'

'There are worse things.' I covered leftover rice pudding with a cloth and carried it home.

Florrie sat in bed knitting a shawl full of holes. Perhaps I'd lived with her too long. Daft as it was, something about her nonsense made sense. I don't need to be a wife to be a parent, she'd said, I can make my own happiness.

'What's so special about Valentino anyway?' I asked, handing her pudding and a spoon. If women have a type, he wasn't mine. He looked like an otter. Slippery, too clean.

Florrie stroked her picture frame, 'He has a beautiful voice.'

'No one's ever heard him,' I said.

'Maybe that's it. I love the silence. I can't imagine him saying a cross word.'

I remembered my father once losing his voice. Words were rationed. Survivalist. Crucial. 'Tea...Bread.' My mother brought in his coffee and he patted her hand. I'd never seen them touch without handing something over, the housekeeping, the salt or pepper, but for a week everything was an 'I love you.' Hands reached through the silence like a space in a wall, until his voice returned.

I could see why a silent man spoke to Florrie more than one who whispered sweet nothings. She was more content on her own than settling for whatever was around. I supposed it didn't hurt.

ON A SATURDAY in late June, I stepped into the ABC without deciding to become a cinema goer. It just happened. Florrie was due any day. She squeezed past the concessions and the lad she once described as boring as toothache. He watched her with a look of combined relief and disappointment, before returning to the popcorn needs of a girl at his side.

'If it's a boy, I'm calling him Rudolph.' Florrie grinned.

I rolled my eyes. There had been plenty of Rudolph's christened that year. Women stood beside taciturn husbands, cradling private daydreams.

'What if it's a girl?'

'I'll call her Valentine.'

We followed the usher down the aisle. The pianist began playing. I perched on my seat. There were a hundred things I could be doing on a sunny day, but here I was.

The screen flickered, and a silver desert rippled. Valentino stared at a shimmering dancing girl. Florrie rested her head on her hand and gazed at the film, lost in the beautiful lies. I was in no position to condemn her. The world was changing. What did I know about life or love? I knew only one: a plain man who married me, let me speak as softly as I liked, filled my life with routine and the sort of love no one makes a fuss about, and finally died. I shifted in my seat. Onscreen, Valentino stepped close to the dancing girl and lifted her hands to his lips. He gazed at her fingers as if wanting to kiss every chore they ever did. He stood over her, breathing her in. The kiss only lasted a second, but he didn't let go. I watched. There was nothing to do but sit in the dark and let the tears roll.

The Silent Woman

Anna Mazzola

DOES HE KNOW I saw it? I cannot tell. He closes the paper and looks at me with a bored sort of hatred, but that is how they always look at me now. To them, I have become an animal, chained; its fur worn away, its eyes dull. There must, though, still be some spark deep within me that they have not killed, because I think I know what I saw.

He wipes his mouth, stands, then moves towards the door, the paper folded in his hand. He says, 'Get on with it, then.'

I am not expected to reply. In two years I have barely spoken, and when I do speak, it must be in English. I am beginning to forget my own language. I am beginning to forget who I am.

THROUGH THE WINDOW, I watch him go. Standing back, so that he cannot see me, I watch as he walks towards his car. I see what he does and I know why he does it. He knows that I can read, though he does not know how well; how I have taught myself in stolen moments from the newspapers they discard. I hear the grumble of the ignition, the whir of the electronic gates opening. As the car drives through, the tall gates slide shut, the gates through which I can never go. I feel a flicker of something, but I cannot make myself do it. Not yet.

Instead, I clear the breakfast plates and I work, as I know I have to, to clean again the floors that I have cleaned every day for the past two years. I have come to hate their whiteness, the hardness of the tiles beneath my knees. I hate the rice that they make me cook and which for two years has been the only thing I have eaten, apart from scraps from their plates. My body has become a different thing, of muscle and sinew and bone and pain; not the soft shape it once was. At night, despite my exhaustion, sometimes sleep does not come. Instead, I lie on the mattress in my narrow room remembering the earth floor of my home, the smell of my children's skin: milk, spice, sweat. It is the memory of their smiles – like sunlight in the darkness – that reminds me I have to live.

As I clean the house, I watch the clock – ten o'clock, half past – I know I must do it soon or it will be too late. He will be back; or she will, and then I will never know. But fear stifles me, stops my breath. For I know all too well what they will do to me if they believe I have disobeyed them again. I still bear the scars, inside and out, from when I tried to scale the gates. That was a long time ago, when I was foolish. In the days that I used to cry. After that, they installed the cameras, the ones that watch me wherever I go.

At least that is what they said. But as I look up at the ceiling, at the walls, I begin to wonder if even that is lies. After all, it has been lies from the first. 'A good job', they told me when I left Benin. Meals. Money to send back to your family. Then days of darkness and dread in the back of a van, cramped and airless with the youngest crying, one dying. When we arrived, they took my passport and my papers and they brought me to work here, unpaid, in the house which has been my prison ever since.

Except it is not truly a prison. Sometimes, when I have not angered them, I am allowed into the little garden. I could shout for help; I could scream. I have imagined it enough times, but I cannot do it. Because it is the fear which is my real cage. The fear of what they have done and will do again. The fear of what will happen to me if I leave here. As they so often remind me, I am in this country without papers, without permission: I am a criminal. If I go to the police, they will lock me up and I will never see my daughters again. I will never see their light brown eyes, hear their laughter. Better, I have thought, to stay silent and hope that one day, when I have worked out the debt that I owe for my passage, they will let me go, as they once told me they would.

But as I watch the minutes on the clock tick by, as I feel the callous on my palm burst and the sharpness of hunger in my stomach, I know they will never let me go. I think I know what I have seen.

At eleven o'clock I collect the rubbish bag from the kitchen and make myself go to the front door. I am simply carrying out my duties, I tell myself. I am committing no wrong. Yet I feel sickness creep through me, a coldness in my bones. For two years I have been told I am nothing. I am not sure I have the strength to try.

But then I am there, in the driveway, in the daylight. I have made it. The stench rises to me as I open the lid of the bin. I see the white of the paper and grab it, dump the rubbish bag, then walk quickly back to the kitchen, my blood roaring in my ears. I sit on the cold white floor. I fumble through the pages until I find what I glimpsed earlier. The sickness is now a shakiness as I see the words, clearer and closer now: 'Jailed for 11 years for modern slavery.'

Modern. Slavery. They are two words I know but I have never seen them together before. There is a picture of a man, his face bloated and pale. I read, slowly, my fingers following the words. I do not understand everything, but I understand enough. This man, he kept people. People like me. People who worked seven days a week for no money, little food. People who were told that if they spoke out they would be imprisoned. But they are not in prison. It is this man with the bloated face who sleeps in a narrow cell.

I read the article again, still not quite believing it is real. Then, carefully, I tear out the page. I fold it over and over and I go to my room, where I hide it beneath my mattress. My lips move in a silent prayer.

FOR THE REST of the afternoon, I continue with my cleaning, my cooking, the routine that I have completed every day for the past two years. But all the time, I feel something growing within me, like tiny green shoots on a dying baobab branch, like the bubbling of the ocean as the wave rises.

I cannot do it yet. I cannot do it today. Maybe not tomorrow either. But soon, soon I will run into the garden and I will shout to the neighbours for help. I will shout and I will scream until they hear my voice. I will see my children again.

Not Our Kind Of Girl

Anne Hamilton

WE'D NEVER HAD much to do with Mrs McVeigh until the summer I turned nine. My granny was supposed to look after me over the long school holidays but she went and broke her hip and ended up in a convalescent home. It was all very inconvenient, my mam fretted, what were we supposed to do now? Mam worked in the Co-op, you see, so it wasn't like I could chum her along, but the way she went on, you'd think gran had done the hip to spite her.

'There's always Mrs McVeigh.' My dad's voice came from behind his paper where he couldn't catch Mam's evil eye.

I held my breath and mimed a Sunday School prayer, *Gentle Jesus, meek and mild, look upon a little child*...Not that I was little anymore but I guessed God or Jesus or whoever was on duty would understand. And they must've, because Mam muttered how beggars couldn't be choosers when they were between a rock and a hard place and she took off her pinny and ran down to Mrs McVeigh for *a word*. When she came back, she had pursed lips, and said, 'You're to be a good girl, mind, and no nonsense.'

I shot off to bed early before she could change her mind, then I made myself comfy listening to her and Dad through the keyhole.

When she finished rattling pans, Mam said, 'It's not a good idea, Frank. She's got notions that one.'

I heard Dad sigh and fold up his *Daily Mirror*. Was it me or Mrs McVeigh who had the notions? Probably her, because I didn't know what they were. Maybe notions were like treasures; Mrs McVeigh definitely had lots of treasures, you could see them through her front window. Mam said they were tat, mucky dust-harbourers, and the least the old woman could do was invest in a decent pair of nets, but I couldn't wait to get my hands on them.

'You worry too much,' my dad said, like he always did (she said he didn't worry enough). 'Mari'll be bored stiff, trotting around after the old girl, doing good deeds and wotnot.'

'It's the wotnot that bothers me.' Mam was rinsing out the tea towel now. 'She's... she's... *dangerous* that woman, Frank. She goes up to that Lilian one at Queer House. They say she helps out...' She quietened to her not-in-front-of-Mari voice, even though I wasn't there. Dangs! I couldn't lean into the keyhole any further, I'd have fallen in the door.

Whatever my mam said made Dad roar. 'What a load of old boll...ards. This is the nineteen-seventies, not the eighteens! She's an old biddy doing what old biddies do. Now, put the telly on and give your old man a cuddle.'

I nearly danced a jig in my nightie. Mrs McVeigh was *dangerous*? And there was a place called *Queer House*? Brillo. Double brillo.

I took out my imagination and polished it.

Mrs McVeigh was a lady Soviet spy.

Mrs McVeigh was a real life Elsie Tanner.

Mrs McVeigh was a white witch...

IF I'M HONEST, it started off less than thrilling. Yes, I got to play with Mrs McVeigh's treasures; she had a set of roundy dolls on the mantelpiece that all fitted inside each other, *Russian* dolls she called them. My ears perked up til she said they were a present 'cause she'd never got further than Scarborough, so I crossed 'spy' off my list. She was no Elsie Tanner either – she didn't even watch *Coronation Street*, if you can imagine that – and she hadn't ever had a husband of her own, let alone stolen somebody else's. She'd not much truck with men, she said, she was only called Mrs because that's what they called all the cooks up at the old infirmary and she'd worked there for years before. 'Before what?' I asked. But she pretended not to hear.

There were no signs of her being a white witch, or even a black one, either.

Then, two Thursdays later, when I skipped down the stair, she already had her hat on and looked, not worried exactly but–

'We're in a wee bit of a boorach,' was what she said. 'Can you keep a secret, Marianne?'

I could, oh, I could. I knew it was a big one because she called me by my Sunday name. I crossed my heart and hoped to die and she clucked my cheek and said there was no need to go that far.

'I've got a friend, called Lilian,' she said as we walked down the street. Yesss! I wanted to punch the air like a boxer; Queer House, here we come. 'She's a bit afeart of the world is Lilian, and that means the world is sometimes a bit afeart of her. Not you.' She squeezed my hand. 'Not a fine big girl like you, but – other people.'

She meant my mam. My mam didn't like anything she decided was dirty or foreign or not lady-like.

'Mari, girl. Stop catching flies!' Mrs McVeigh poked my shoulder but in a friendly way. I could see that she was worried about trusting me and I needed to think right quick. I wasn't allowed to tell untruths, which was probably the one thing in the world Mam and Mrs McVeigh agreed on, but I knew a way to keep everyone happy.

'Silence is golden.' I put my fingers to my lips.

Mrs McVeigh nodded briskly enough to shake out a hat pin. 'You'll go far, madam, you will,' she said.

I liked that. We didn't go far from home, I'd not even been to Scarborough. I'd never been out of Scotland.

We stopped off at the chemist where Mrs McVeigh scared off spotty-faced Cammy and made him hand over a pile of mysterious boxes – 'Never you mind,' she said to me before I'd even opened my mouth – and then we stopped at the laundry and the grocer. Mrs McVeigh's trolley was getting hard to pull over the cobbles and my face was red taking turns with her. She gave me a toffee to keep my strength up.

When she eventually said, 'Here we are,' my mouth was dryer than a brewer's armpit like my dad says when he's thirsty for beer. I was dreaming of a bottle of cold pop but I soon got distracted. Well, I thought, whatever Lilian was afeart of, it hadn't kept her short. Queer House was one of those fancy tall and skinny houses in the New Town.

'Why's it even called Queer House? It's not queer at all.' The words got out before I could stop them.

'What's that? How did you–? Oh.' I could see Mrs McVeigh's brain ticking over. 'It's Creare House, Mari, not Queer. It's 'creation' in Latin…' She didn't sound very sure, but she pushed on. 'Lilian is very clever. A true scholar and help-meet.'

I thought she sounded too good to be true. Or a bit of

a joker. I mean, a queer house was a million times better than a creation house. I scuffed my shoe and kicked a loose bit of dirt into the road.

Anyway, we went round the back and rang the kitchen door bell. The lady who opened it was as tall and thin as the building, with hair falling out of its clips, and she had on a blue pinny. She looked like a wanting scullery maid from *Upstairs Downstairs*. I nearly fell over when Mrs McVeigh called her Lilian.

'This is Marianne, Lilian,' Mrs M said, stepping inside. 'She'll sit quietly in the kitchen and fold napkins, won't you, Mari?'

'Yes,' I said, meaning no.

Lilian said, 'Hello, dear. My, what a help you'll be.'

I'd been wrong; she was *Upstairs* posh. Kind, though, in a loopy way.

I was angling for a good nose around – this was the poshest house I'd ever been in, everybody I knew, except Uncle Bryan and Mr King who had an upper villa, lived in a tenement flat – but neither of them took the hint. The kitchen was probably as big as our flat without anything shiny or new in it, though, but the passage to the front room, what Lilian called the drawing room, had a real statue in it, like a museum. Even better, the downstairs lav had a picture of a nude fat lady laying on a settee; I couldn't pee but for looking at her. I practised her pouty lips all morning until Mrs McVeigh asked me why I had a face that looked as if it'd sucked lemons.

Nobody was telling me anything, but I decided Lilian ran a boarding house, an odd one, right enough. The guests were heard – soft footsteps, closing doors, I even caught voices – but not seen by me, however many times I needed to go back to the lavvy or begged to carry the tea tray to the front room. They also seemed to use more bed sheets than even my mam needed to be hygienic. Towels too; Mrs McVeigh's trolley was deeper than Mary Poppins' bag. Maybe Lilian's company was poorly, I thought. Maybe it was a convalescent home for people with 'nerves.' That would explain the chemist visits and Lilian's locked medicine cupboard.

'Does Lilian run a boarding house?' I asked Mrs McVeigh on the way home. She didn't answer, she just sped across the road. I skipped along beside her. 'Or is it a nursing home?' She still couldn't hear, so I said it louder.

'Not so's you'd notice,' was all I got.

'Can we go back again?' I changed tack; I'd have to work out the mystery myself.

'We'll see,' she said. 'Any more questions?' Her eyebrows were up like a school teacher so I knew she meant I'd better not have.

***

WE WENT ONCE a week after that.

I liked Lilian and Mrs McVeigh, and I was soon fairly

sure that they weren't dangerous and nor was Queer House queer. And I never did see Lilian's company, hard as I tried. Then, the last Thursday, it all changed.

This time Lilian was waiting at the open door, more scatty-looking than ever; whatever Mrs McVeigh had said that first time, I didn't think Lilian was afeart of anything outside, she was just too busy running around after her ghostly guests.

'Trouble brewing?' Mrs McVeigh said to Lilian, and squinted her eye at me to show she was talking in code.

'Every five minutes, give or take.' Lilian looked as if she'd just run a race and come last; exhausted and sad. 'There are... complications. You'll need to run out to the phone box.'

'*What?* Are you sure–'

'Now, Mrs McVeigh. Please.'

'Mind yourself, missy,' Mrs McVeigh said to me before she scooted.

I was surprised. Bonkers Lilian really was the real boss of... whatever it was.

'What's happening? Who's she calling? What is *that?*' It sounded like a werewolf howling at a whole solar system of moons, and it stopped me tugging at Lilian's sleeve.

'I must go,' she said and hurried for the door.

'But–' The devil noise repeated itself and I screamed.

Lilian came back and knelt down in front of me. 'It's

alright, Mari. There's nothing to worry about.' She put her hand under my chin. 'Look at me, good girl. Did Mrs McVeigh tell you I was a doctor? No? Well, I was, up in the infirmary. And now, I like to look after people here. I have a young lady, three young ladies, actually, staying with me... You might like to call them my... my nieces.'

'And one is ill?' Lilian was a lady doctor; I couldn't believe it. Okay, she was nice, and like Mrs McVeigh said, cleverer than she looked, but I still wouldn't want her taking out my tonsils.

'She does need to go to the hospital. I think she needs an operation.' Lilian stood up. She looked sad again. 'I have to look after her until the ambulance arrives. Please stay here, Marianne.'

It was an order, but then again, there was a real life ambulance coming. I weighed up possible punishments, then thought, oh sod it, like my dad says but shouldn't. I put my hands over my ears, just in case the screeching started again, and crept through the hall.

Mrs McVeigh came panting back at the same time as I heard the nee-na and flashing blue lights turned the corner. The stiff front door was opened, and two ambulance men carried a stretcher in. I crept across, and only peeked out into the hall to see how they would manage to carry the poorly niece down the stairs, but they didn't. All I saw was a fat girl with a red face heaving herself along and moaning, and they stuck her on the stretcher on the bottom.

Lilian took off her pinny and reached for her coat, which was on the bannister, but one of the ambulance men touched her arm and said, 'Best not, eh? Leave her to us.'

She drooped like a willow-tree. 'I'm needed here, anyway,' she said and looked away from the fat girl and up the stairs.

I followed her eyes, and there were two more girls up there, both of them were huddled up, crying. It was weird that Lilian had such fat nieces when she was a beanpole.

'You've probably saved this one's life, Dr McLennon, and the bairn's. Look at it that way,' said the nice ambulance man but his friend just grunted. He was scowling at the groaning niece; I wouldn't want to carry her either. She looked like she weighed a tonne and she wasn't laying a bit still. She tossed the blanket off her belly and I'm sure I saw blood, or maybe it was sauce from her black-pudding and bacon breakfast on the hem of her dressing-gown. It was the kind of sight my mam would hurry me away from.

'I try to save all of them,' Lilian whispered, but probably I was the only one who heard her under the sound of the door closing. I had to think very fast just then; get to the lavvy for an alibi before they noticed I wasn't in the kitchen.

***

WE DIDN'T GO back to Queer House again, me and Mrs McVeigh. Lilian said better not to. We didn't talk about it either. *I* knew not to and they didn't know what I'd seen. We stayed in Mrs M's flat, and all the while I sucked on the secret I didn't understand as if it were a sherbet lemon.

Then, in the last week of the school holidays, Mam came home, raging and shook me.

'Where did Mrs McVeigh take you?'

'Ouch,' I said. Like Brownies taught me, I was prepared; you had to be when you lived with my mam. 'Stop it. She took me to the chemist and the laundry and the grocer. She told me not to tell you...'

'What?' My mam was this far from exploding.

'...that I got a free sticky lolly from spotty Cammy.'

Dad got the earful. There was a lot of pursed lips and phrases like, 'not our sort of girl,' and, 'the type that go on marches.' The world was a shambles, she said.

'Give it a rest, old girl,' Dad said, after a bit. 'Different strokes for different folks, is all.' He pointed his knife at his plate. 'One man's mince and tatties is another's steak tartare, eh, Mari?'

I had to go with her to work, after that, even though it was frowned upon. In the backroom of the Co-op, I ate a lot of broken biscuits and read all the week-old comics. I missed Mrs McVeigh; she'd vanished overnight, so maybe she was a witch, after all. Perhaps she and Lilian had just got rid of the poorly nieces and gone on another trip to Scarborough.

Then I saw it. I'd finished my library book and the comics, so I was bored, that's why I looked at the old newspapers. Guess what? Right there on the front page of one was Queer House. It really was. It took me ages to spell out the big, black print. It said, 'Girls In Trouble: unofficial unmarried mothers' home under scrutiny,' and the writing underneath read, 'Is Creare House creating a new world – or destroying it? See our feature, page 4.'

I ripped out both pages and stuffed them in my knickers.

IT WAS LIKE a jigsaw with bits missing, and I'm not sure I've ever fully pieced it together. Years later, packing up my belongings to leave home and start nursing training, I rediscovered that newspaper cutting, and wondered, again, about Mrs McVeigh and Lilian. Even then, I never brought it up with my mother; for her, right and wrong, nice and nasty, were, and always would be, black and white. My shades of grey meant we clashed. A lot.

Dangerous, she'd called them. And even in the snapshot I'd seen, Lilian and Mrs McVeigh *were* dangerous. They were bold and fearless, and they were trying to create a better, fairer world for those stigmatised young women under Lilian's care. Back then, I'd wanted to be brave and different, accepting and without judgement – all those things – too. But I was just a little girl, who had only just begun to grasp that her poor Mam's 'taste' was discrimination, pure and simple. I still remember vowing that one day, I would be strong. I'd go into a red telephone box and I'd come out as Wonder Woman, but like Mrs McVeigh and Lilian, I'd be all the more powerful because I wouldn't be in costume and nobody would see me coming.

One day I would change the world so that a girl, or a boy, could be any sort they wanted. I'm still trying.

Thank you, Mrs McVeigh and Lilian, whoever you were, and wherever you are.

Treading On Needles

Dane Divine

THE WITCH TRIED to warn me.

'If you walk in his world, each step will hurt you like treading on needles and you'll lose your tongue.'

'But I love him,' I replied.

'He's so different, princess. If he marries another, you'll be just foam on the water.'

'He told me, he loves me.'

She sighed so deeply, it sounded as if her heart had crumpled deep in her chest. Still she handed me the potion. Inside a bottle the colour of octopus ink, it was as thick and red as human blood. It filled my mouth with a salty, coppery tang as I swallowed it down.

'Thank you,' I said.

She cried as I left.

***

I FOUND HIM on the edge of the worlds, where the sea meets the land.

'You came.' He smiled.

***

'I LOVE YOUR legs,' he said as he stroked my skin.

'They're all yours,' I said, gasping as my girlhood seeped away in pain, blood and salt water.

***

'SING TO ME, like you did from the sea,' he'd say. And each night, as the orange embers huddled and glowed, I'd sing my prince to sleep and he'd dream of the mermaid in his arms.

Watching him there, as I stroked his hair, dreaming of our loving and our kissing, I thought of how wrong the witch had been.

***

'HOW DO YOU manage that?' he'd say as I'd bring him back fish from the sea.

'It's nothing you can't learn,' I'd reply, settling down beside him to gut them.

'How do you manage that?' I'd say as he'd rekindle the flames of the fire, which kept us warm at night.

'It's nothing you can't learn.' He'd laugh, settling down beside me to feel the heat on my skin.

***

'I NEED TO go back,' he said one morning, standing up and moving away.

'I'll come with you.'

'But,' he started, looking me up and down.

I felt a sharp tingling in my soles.

'I suppose with some good clothes...' He kissed me. 'After all, you are very beautiful.'

***

HIS CASTLE WAS as lovely as my own. They let us through the gates. I was taken away, across the square to be powdered and dressed.

***

'BUT, WHERE'S MY prince?' I asked, rubbing at my sore feet.

'He's in court with the queen and the king. He said he will see you as soon as he is allowed.'

I waited all day.

At night he returned.

'Princess, where are your pretty legs?' He laughed, seeing me in the gown. He hurried to untie it and found the legs he loved so much.

'You should be with me always,' he murmured. 'Tomorrow I'll have them find you more suitable clothes and I'll show you my lands.'

'I want to see everything.'

'And so you shall, my little foundling princess.'

'But you asked me to leave the sea for you. We found each other,' I replied.

'Yes, yes, you silly thing, but that is what they are all calling you and I quite like it.'

My feet hurt.

***

TOGETHER WE RODE on his horse all through his lands, which were as rich and expansive as my own seas.

'I love to travel with you.'

'It's fun, but my parents have arranged a gathering soon. We must prepare you for that. You mustn't appear too... strange.'

'But I am a mer-princess. To me, some of your land ways are strange.'

'Just do it,' he said, trying to rub the frown from my forehead with his thumb. 'Try not to be so... you.'

I half remembered something the witch had said, but his kisses pushed it away.

***

THE FOLLOWING WEEK the maids instructed me on how to hold the peculiar eating utensils. They positioned me in the art of sitting and standing, and attempted to teach me to curtsey.

'But I am a mer-princess. This is how we would do

this in my court.'

They merely shook their heads and said, 'Just try harder.'

'Where is my prince?' I demanded after one of them slapped my hands as I'd spilt some soup from my spoon.

'Probably entertaining the guests.'

'Are they here already?'

'Of course,' they replied, digging the needles in deeper and deeper.

***

'GOOD EVENING, FOUNDLING,' he said. 'I have been asked to escort you to the ball.'

I reached to kiss his well-known lips. He turned and let me take his arm.

Each step drew blood.

***

THE HALL WAS filled with humans. As the music played, they moved gracefully, like a colourful shoal.

'We must dance,' he said.

As we swayed around the floor, his body once more next to mine, with the sharpness of each step, I began to cry.

'Stop crying,' he hissed.

'I've missed you and I miss my sisters.' I sniffed. 'They would love this ball. It's so beautiful.'

'Well, don't make a scene. It's embarrassing.'

***

'MOTHER, FATHER, PLEASE meet the foundling,' he said.

'She is not one of us.'

'Mother,' he retorted, but the acceptance in his tone pushed the needles deep within me.

'I am a mer-princess,' I said.

'Yes, indeed.' They replied, dismissing me.

They continued, berating their son. 'Think of your position.'

'I am a mer-princess,' I said, asserting my substance. 'Our marriage would bring a union of land and sea. We have food and treasures to share.'

'Yes, indeed.'

'Our neighbour's daughter is a preferable match.'

My prince merely nodded.

I was reduced to a happy summer on the beach.

***

I LEFT AND walked to the sea. Waves pushed angrily against the harbour walls. I felt their fluid-rage deep within me. I was a mer-princess. I deserved an equal.

I jumped.

The water quickly found my skin. The clothes, suddenly wet and heavy, dragged me down. As I sank, I felt hands untying them, taking them off.

'You okay, Your Highness?' asked the witch.

'I will be,' I said, opening my gills.

'Welcome back.'

She handed me a potion. I drank it without a thought. And, flicking my tail, we swam home.

The Second Brain
Cath Bore

IT'S HOT. KATIE Morris and me are in a big plastic paddling pool at the back of her house. Katie's mum is inside drinking coffee with my mum. I can see them through the kitchen window if I stretch out my neck far enough. Who'd have hot drinks in this weather? They seem happy though, chatting on the other side of the glass. We splash about in the water turning the soil around the paddling pool black, the blades of grass going all shiny. We're making loads of noise. I'm wearing my swimming costume with sunflowers down the front. It's my favourite.

Katie's dad appears right out of nowhere. He's in a suit and tie and carries a leather briefcase with sharp corners. He seems ready to tell us to be quiet but says 'What's all this then?' Kneels on the wet patch of lawn, his briefcase slapping on the ground as it falls over onto its side.

Katie's smile stills, goes all fixed and tinny, a strip of

white teeth between stretched thinned lips. She won't look at me as his signet ring with an oval black stone in the middle presses against my skin. The gold is as warm as blood. His face is sweaty. I hold my breath and the sunflower on my front shrinks to tiny and blazes so bright I reckon you can make it out from space, never mind the kitchen metres away. But no one comes. Butterflies flutter in my stomach and I try not to notice his knuckles and the metal and how everything apart from him is now so still and quiet. Instead I think hard and worry about how he'll end up with grass stains on his pants. They'll show when he finishes and as he gets to his feet but I hope not because everyone will know and Mrs Morris will have extra washing.

'There's no need to be shy, you can't be shy once you start school.' Mum's hand on the small of my back pushes me forward to say "thank you for having me". The butterflies go mad.

'Not long to go now,' says Mrs Morris. 'Until school.'

'Not long,' echoes Mum. 'September.'

I thought butterflies only live for one day but that's not true. They return every time I see Mr and Mrs Morris and Katie or even think about them. But it isn't excited butterflies, the nice ones that tickle and wriggle about and make me look forward to something. With these butterflies, their wings flap like they're angry with me. And they hurt like anything.

At school the butterflies are with me a lot. But secondary school is where I really find out about them. Who they are and what they want.

'The body hides a second brain. It's in your stomach. There are 100 million neurons lining your stomach and gut. Together they are called "the little brain".' Mrs Parkinson the biology teacher waves her hands as she speaks. 'The neurons keep in contact with the brain in your skull via the vagus nerves. The vagus nerves influence our emotional state, control our mood or appetite.'

Liam Crossley always sits at the back of the class with Ben Adams and a lad called Damon. Liam screws up his face and they do as well. 'What's that to do with butterflies?'

There's a butterfly chart on the classroom wall. It's got pencil drawings of wet larvae and a giant crispy brown chrysalis as well as different types of butterfly. The cabbage white's wings are round and clean and soft but there are others I don't see in my garden at home or anywhere else. The comma butterfly has ridges along the edges of its wings. The peacock ones are red and bold with sharp curves. I picture them doing the most damage, the spiked tips scraping out my stomach lining. 'Cos that's what it feels like when they kick off inside me.

'Butterflies are an indication of the brain in the stomach talking to the brain in your head,' adds Mrs Parkinson.

'Oh.' Liam rolls his eyes. His eyes are ever so blue and he's got blond hair and a clean face. Everyone at school fancies Liam. I fancy him too until one day when I'm stood right behind him in the queue at lunchtime. He turns around and beckons with his finger for me to come close, and when I lean forward barely believing my luck he hits me with a question. I'm standing there holding a plastic tray with a portion of spaghetti bolognese and a carton of blackcurrant juice, the type you put the straw through the top, and everybody hears what he asks me. The school kills itself laughing. The room fills with hyenas, ones Mrs Parkinson showed us in a documentary once. The butterflies in my stomach go hysterical. Liam asks me again. I don't know what the right answer is.

Should I have said something to him, perhaps? I practise that night in my bedroom, in the mirror. 'I feel uncomfortable, you saying that.' I read in a magazine that's what you need to say when there's something not quite right. But I sound unconvincing to my own ears and the butterflies cause a right fuss as I force the words out through my lips. I hug myself and bend over, my spine curved like a giant letter C, hoping to crush their wings and make them go still. I repeat the sentence to myself, my accent thickens and broadens and goes slow and awkward but I tell myself that when I'm older I'll be able to say it properly and out loud to people.

But I never do. At my bar job at uni – doing a biology

degree by the way – two men, regulars, bring out a copy of The Sun newspaper as I wash their dirty beer glasses. They wonder out loud about Chloe from Bedford on Page Three. My nipples are bigger, they guess, and a darker brown.

'I feel uncomfortable.' I'm in the cool of the ladies' toilets. I hope my words travel along the walls and soak into the carpet fibres, float through the air and slide into the men's brains, shutting them up. Only it doesn't work. I read from my Kindle on my break and one of them shouts "are you reading 50 Shades?" for no bloody reason whatsoever. No one reads that anymore. I pretend to ignore him, both of them, and concentrate on the words onscreen but go over the same line of dialogue loads of times, my eyes sliding left to right because the really gobby man keeps on repeating the question.

Jamie the bar manager tells them to "ease off, lads" and they nod.

But me, what do I do? I don't tell them to mind their own business; I let the butterfly wings shred my insides instead.

I wish I'd got up and shouted, made them shut the fuck up. That's because it might have helped me when Jamie gets on my train after the pub closes, chatting about nonsense. I feel stupid asking "why are you here?" and by the time he's walked me home ("I don't want you walking home alone," he says) it seems rude to send him away. He stands there with his hands in his pockets making "brrr it's cold" gestures although it is really quite mild, if a little damp. When we go in my house he kisses me. My stomach is bulky with squabbling butterflies. I want to say "I feel uncomfortable" as he licks the roof of my mouth and the sides of my teeth and I tell myself that when he takes his tongue back, I'll say as much. But when it eventually happens, he asks straight off if he's a good kisser and I tell him "yeah, 'course".

He smiles. I smile too. He stays all weekend, rings in work sick. I let him have sex with me loads of times and each time, butterflies fight harder in my stomach. The edges of their wings slash and stab and make me bleed. I don't know how to find the words to stop them, to make them go still. Saying "I feel uncomfortable" doesn't seem to fit. Not after I've said how great the sex is and what's good about it. And Jamie wants to know, each and every time. Why does he want to know? He looks hurt when I pause for too long before answering. There are plenty of reasons to say how awful it all is for me but it's never the right time, somehow, circumstances falling short, conditions never perfect. And Jamie, he won't hear me anyway. I'm thinking the butterflies do, though. When I say "I feel uncomfortable" silently in my head they go off on one and let me know about it, big time. I'm thinking now the butterflies are the only ones listening to me, the only ones who can hear. I don't have to do anything, just think and they appear. I'm starting to believe the butterflies aren't bad after all. I'm starting to feel they stir because they want me to run. Maybe they are my friends. They may as well be, because they're always here no matter what and I don't think they're leaving me anytime soon.

I don't want them to, now I think on. And the more I accept it, the more I see them and the more I want them with me. I didn't know this, but butterflies flock to sunflowers keenly because they are so bright. Fancy that. So in spring I plant sunflowers in my garden. The malty hum of nectar and the broad flat flower heads bring more and more butterflies to me over the months and soon I've got a butterfly garden. The air is full of them, and all the colours. They're good company. But when winter comes and the butterflies with the pretty wings are gone, I actually don't mind so much. The winter brings with it a cold that forces everything flat and still, and safe and in its bloody place and where it should be and where I can see it. And anyway, as the temperatures dip and as the leaves crisp and fall and the branches of trees blacken and I can see my own breaths, the butterflies are still inside me, warning me where I cannot go.

The Servitude Of The Sudaarp
Taria Karrilion

Alien Cultures Test Paper

** Complete as many answers as you can before the second sun sets. **

** The use of night-vision or telepathic technology is strictly forbidden. **

Q1. NAME the newly-discovered Alien World that has a multi-gendered, non-religious caste-system.

The Planet of the Sudaarp

Q2. GIVE A DETAILED EXAMPLE of how the indigenous species of that world is divided.

The Sudaarp are divided into ~~four~~ two genders – the WOTHs and the SAHMs.

The WOTHs are mostly hunters, farmers, labourers or machine operators. They usually have greater physical strength, a more aggressive nature, are highly territorial and can be fiercely protective of their immediate and regional tribe.

The SAHMs (often semi-habitat-based, multi-skilled and caregivers) are slightly smaller with longer pelts, feeding ~~tubes~~ glands for their infants, also very protective, and are rumoured to have additional ~~antennae~~ eyes in the back of their skulls.

Q3. STATE whether IERA (the Interplanetary Equal Rights Alliance) have deemed this a fair division. Provide detailed examples.

The IERA recently declared the Sudaarp culture to be unfairly divided for numerous reasons, including:

☐ On many of the planet's continents, SAHMs are excluded from many social rights and opportunities, including adequate healthcare, education, ~~grouping~~ partnering liberties and care in old age.

☐ In many WOTH/SAHM mated partnerships, the SAHMs are left to raise the young alone, preventing them from earning an adequate income, as the Sudaarp Rulers make deeply inadequate provision for the care of Sudaarp dependents, both young and elderly. (Occasionally a WOTH is placed in this position, but this is far rarer).

☐ The WOTHs receive greater rewards for their labours per orbital rotation, whereas the SAHMs are penalised (by their nurturing role) because being semi-habitat-based often prevents them from maintaining – or progressing into – adequately paid roles.

☐ Further to this, the Sudaarp operate a much lower pay rate for SAHMs, known as 'Servitude Season', which the IERA has deemed 'grossly unjust'. Servitude Season lasts for a sixth of the planet's year when SAHMs work for no payment. To date, no evidence has been recorded as to why this system continues to be accepted.

Q4. *LIST three other ways in which the planet's Rulers restrict the SAHMs freedoms.*

☐ Fewer SAHMs in positions of Authority, which has produced a highly WOTH-dominated society, even though the two gender groups are of nearly equal numbers.

☐ In some regions, SAHMs are not allowed out in public without their entire bodies and faces being covered, while in others near nudity is freely allowed. In all regions, regardless of clothing traditions, violent SAHM abuse is sometimes tolerated, with the victim even being blamed for inviting the attack.

☐ The rulers of some sub-groups allow the practice of ritual mutilation of SAHMs, causing disfigurement, disease and life-long suffering. There appears to be no rational reason for this practice which violates the Fundamental Entity Rights Accord.

Q5. *NAME the three rebel SAHM groups and the varying severity of their practices.*

☐ The Pacifists – operate by calm, eloquent protests and petitions. Want to prove their ability to campaign unemotionally and strictly within the law. Never violent.

☐ The Lobbyists – make organised appeals to the Sudaarp rulers by petition and legal campaigns. Have a higher profile and will break protest laws to property only.

☐ The Radicals (a breakaway faction from the Lobbyists) – this group takes high profile, violent action to promote their Cause. Led by the now deceased Melpanen K'shuratei, who spearheaded the campaign for SAHM Rights Awareness by sacrificing herself to the stampeding Seroh beast of the Sudaarp Ruler in full view of a vast public gathering.

Q6. *Based on your knowledge of other primitive alien cultures, which of the following factors would be necessary for the Sudaarp to earn membership of the Interplanetary Equal Rights Alliance?*

[   ] *Gender equality via co-operative survival of an apocalyptic event.*

[   ] *Forcible reprogramming by seeding the atmosphere with mind-altering nanites.*

[X] *Covert placement of our own Educators disguised as poets / authors / musicians.*

[   ] *This species is too primitive and unjust to ever be acceptable to IERA.*

Q7. *By what other names is Sudaarp known? Full marks will only be given for the correct spelling in the primary native language of the Sudaarp.*

☐ *Sol 3*

☐ *Terra*

☐ *E-A-R-T-H*

Out Of Office

Emily Kerr

To: j.smith@biz.com
From: j.smythe@biz.com
Re: Out of Office

Hi Jasper

Thanks for your email. As you will have seen, my Out of Office notification is on, so I guess we could say that strictly I'm under no obligation to reply to you. However, we're mates, and as you know, I'm a diligent soul, so I feel I should send some kind of response. After all, I know you'll have been surprised at receiving an Out of Office when I'm clearly still sitting here at the desk opposite you. There, I just gave you a little wave from behind my piles of paperwork, and you looked very confused because you've not received this reply yet. You'll understand in a minute, I hope.

You're absolutely correct, I'm not actually on leave. But the thing is, technically I could be if I wanted to. Admittedly it would be *unpaid* leave. Let me explain…

I want you to cast your mind back to five years ago when we first arrived here. Remember? You had that dodgy little goatee and I was sporting a dip-dye job which my friends really should have advised me against. So, there we were, fresh out of Uni, proud holders of identical degrees, both survivors of several unpaid internships and minimum wage jobs. We were eager and excited worker bees with matching CVs and equally unfortunate hairstyles, looking forward to climbing the career ladder in our chosen profession. I was thrilled to have been offered a job here. I couldn't believe my luck in getting my dream role, just months after graduating. When we were being given the induction on our first day, you confessed you were just as thrilled.

The boss settled us down at these two desks. Identical chairs, matching laptops, the same kind of drawers lurking underneath for us to bash our unwary knees on. We struggled our way through the same mandatory online training, both groaning at being quizzed on the company's policy on everything from recycling to refusing bribes. And then, at last, we got started on some actual work. We were paired up for our first project and the boss asked you to report back on how we got on. I was sneakily a little bit relieved about that, because my first impression of our illustrious leader was that he was pretty scary with his staccato speech and no-nonsense glares.

By project number two, we'd both found our feet at the firm. Gruff attitude from the boss didn't frighten me anymore, and I was determined to show my worth. Now I was the one to report back on our progress. I noticed that this time though, you also got summoned into the meetings and asked for your input. I didn't mind. We were both contributors, and I was pleased we were making an impact on the powers-that-be with our hard graft.

We continued this way for a while, project after project, taking it in turns to be the leader. But I started to get a niggling feeling at the back of my mind. It wasn't something that I could exactly put my finger on, just this sense that in order to make the same impression as you, I had to run, while you got away with strolling. I told myself I was being silly and over-sensitive. Of course, I was valued as much as you. We had the same job titles, same responsibility, we did the same work.

We've often laughed over how much confusion our near-identical email addresses have caused. It's not surprising people get us mixed up. J. Smith and J. Smythe do after all perform exactly the same function within the company. But not so long ago, I received an email intended for you, which made me realise that we're not as similar as I thought we were.

I apologise for reading what you'll soon realise was a confidential exchange, but I'm going to blame HR for messing up. Because they really, really shouldn't have let me see that email. That simple epistle hammered home the fact that my life might be quite different if I'd been born a Jasper like you, rather than a Jenny. It was an email of congratulations, informing you that you've been awarded another pay increase for your hard work. Well done, by the way, I agree that you totally deserve it.

It was the word "another" that really shocked me. Because I've never received a pay increase in all the five years I've worked here. But, I'm equally responsible for the success of our projects. I got the same development review rating as you and, without wishing to sound like I'm blowing my own trumpet, my name was also on that industry award we won this summer.

I scrolled further down, and again I'm sorry that I'm now privy to deeply personal information about you, but I made another disappointing discovery. Way back on that day when we both started here, even then we weren't as identical as I thought we were. Your pay packet was fatter than mine.

So, I've done a few sums and I realised that from today (that's the 3rd November in case you weren't sure) I'm essentially working for free. Hence my little protest against the system with my Out of Office.

All things being equal, I should be starting on that new project this afternoon. But as they aren't, I think I might pop home early. Why not? I'm on my time now, and actually, it feels quite liberating!

See you tomorrow. Maybe.

Jenny x

Gristle

Angela Clarke

I MET TONY on Facebook. Well, that's not actually true. He and I both commented on a photo Belinda Sharpe posted. A lovely shot of the smiling children at the local school receiving their cheque. And he said how much he'd enjoyed talking to me at the Operatic Society's Annual Fundraiser. His profile picture didn't give me much of a clue: it was him in silhouette against a beautiful rocky bay. But he must have been the tall, dark gentleman Candice Duvall introduced me to near the sushi bar. To be honest I'd been trying to reach the Ladies at the point Candice collared me. I was wearing a ball gown I hadn't worn since Jim passed, and I'd forgotten how long it took to extract myself from the necessary underwear. I was on a deadline, so to speak. I remember shaking lots of hands and delivering the repeated perfunctory small talk that goes with these events. *Thank you for your kind words. Yes, I am very proud that Jim's legacy has saved the local library. We must do lunch soon.* Head tilt, sympathetic hand pat, and they're gone.

Funny how you can be surrounded by so many people and still be lonely. I told Jim's photo that night I was still angry he'd left me. That I still missed him. Then I cuddled the cats and had a good cry. I shouldn't have drunk champagne on an empty stomach. So, I was startled when Tony said he'd found me engaging. I hadn't felt engaging. Not for a long time. And I didn't think it would be terrible to accept this man's friend request.

I want to assure you I'm not reckless about the internets. I read the papers. I know about the scams those Nigerian princes try to pull. And poor Valerie Taylor got into a terrible pickle when a nice US army officer she'd been chatting too sent her a very forward photo. She couldn't be sure, but she felt that that part of his anatomy didn't look very American. She suspected he was a Russian spy. I don't know what a Russian spy would want from Valerie, but by that point she had the Rotary Club rapt with the story and I didn't like to interrupt. I only joined Facebook because of Isabelle and the girls. I do the Skype-ing with them a couple of times a week. Every parent hopes their daughter will meet a lovely husband, and Riku is perfection, but Japan is quite far away for your family to be. Seeing Isabelle's updates reduces that distance. Marjorie Phipps says social media is all photos of people's lunch, but I quite like seeing Naomi and Hana eating their breakfast and all dressed for school – it makes me feel like I'm not missing so much. And, yes, I know I should go and visit them. But Jim and I had been planning that trip when he got sick. We postponed it for his treatment. And then of course when things got worse, Isabelle had to fly back anyway. And, well, we never did take it. When I think of stepping onto that plane without him my heart feels like it might break afresh.

Oh dear, I knew this would happen. As soon as I start to talk about Tony, I really start talking about Jim. He was such a wonderful husband. Yes, there were certainly times when I wished he didn't keep absolutely everything in the garage 'in case it was useful'. And that he'd occasionally put me and Isabelle ahead of work. But that's just the kind of man he was: constantly driven to prove himself.

Tony was different. Nights have been the hardest since Jim passed, but Tony always seemed to be awake and happy to chat online. We had so much in common. Soon we were messaging daily. Long streams of conversations. We clicked. We planned to meet at Milly Macclesfield's fundraiser for her Cambodian orphanage, but he wasn't able to make it at the last minute. I was both disappointed and a bit relieved, if I'm honest. It's one thing talking to a man online but actually in person? Jim would have called me a daft old girl, but I felt like I was being unfaithful to our marriage.

It was a few weeks before I felt brave enough to try

again. This time I arranged to meet Tony at the new café opposite the library Jim sponsored. I'd lost weight since Jim passed, so I bought a new dress and got my hair and nails done for the first time in over a year. I was marvelling at how pulled together I looked when he walked in. Not the tall man Candice Duvall had introduced me too, or not as I remembered him. He was blonde for a start, though very handsome in his shirt and waistcoat. Shorter than Jim, around five eight, and a good ten years younger than me. He swept me into a hug and said how wonderful it was to see me and how marvellous my new hair looked. And I wondered if he might be a homosexual, you know? Because Jim would never had noticed if I'd got my hair done. And I relaxed, because if he was that way inclined then this was nothing more than friendship.

We chatted until coffee became lunch. Then we met again for dinner the next day. He insisted on paying, even when I protested. He told me he was a composer. Used to working in the evenings from the years of piano bar gigs and concerts in his youth, he now always composed at night. I told him it was very glamourous and exciting compared to our family pie business. He laughed and said in reality it was quite dull, but he liked that I thought he was glamourous.

I was so convinced he was gay it was a shock when he kissed me. And even more of a shock when I kissed back. It had been so long since I'd felt a man's lips on mine, felt his hands hold me. I'm embarrassed to confess my body responded of its own accord. There was no time to think about Jim, or Isabelle, or anyone else. It was just the two of us. And Tony was sweet and considerate. We took things slowly for my sake. He was a very talented lover. Those piano playing fingers.

Soon he was staying at mine five nights out of seven. And I was like a new woman. No, I was like my old self. Alight with life again. I still talked to Jim's photo, but now I told him about the future, not the past.

When Tony told me about the job in Los Angeles I thought that was it. He was going to be scoring a film for a studio over there, and would need to be on site for eighteen months. This was his big break into the American market, and I knew from Jim and I's own experience that it was in the US that things really got serious. Tony wasn't planning to go for simply eighteen months, he was planning to stay there. Hopefully this film would be the first of many. When he showed me photos of his new house in the hills with its infinity pool overlooking LA I was so happy for him, and so sad for what might have been. Then he asked me to go with him.

Now, for a woman who hasn't been able to get on a plane since her husband died this sounds ridiculous. But being with Tony had resurrected me. His love gave me hope again. Everything would be all right in the end. And really, what did I have keeping me here? No family. My friends are mostly charity contacts; besides, I knew I could do the Skype-ing if I felt I was missing Valerie Taylor's latest drama. I could get pet passports for the cats. This was a chance to really start living again. To make new memories. To make Jim proud. There was one sticky point in the plan: the business.

I'LL ADMIT, I'D let things slide since Jim had been sick. But now I took renewed interest in the board and what they were up to. And I didn't like what I found. Changes had been made to the pension provisions for staff. Contracted holiday days had been reduced. I went to visit Mickey who'd been with Jim from the start. And he told me he'd noticed a change in the quality of the product coming off the line. They were using cheaper meat. Bulking up with gristle. And when he'd raised concerns about the nutrition – *the actual nutrition, god forgive me, Jim* – he'd been made redundant. I have never been so ashamed in all my life as in that moment sitting in Mickey's lounge. I asked why he hadn't come to me. Mickey said he hadn't wanted to intrude at what he'd called a difficult time. Of course, he knew nothing about Tony, and I felt so guilty. Mickey told me he often thought of how Jim had persuaded his dad to take him on at the butcher's shop. *How mighty meat pies grew from small piles of mince.* That was always one of Jim's favourite sayings. Mickey assured me he was grateful for the forty-two years Jim had given him and not to worry. He was sure he'd get another lucky break and find a job real soon.

I came home from that meeting and wept in Tony's arms. Tony couldn't bear to see me so upset. He soothed me. Comforted me. Told me it wasn't my fault. That it was too much to expect me to take over the business from Jim. But his lovely words made little difference. I was the one who had let Mickey down. I had let our customers down, and, worst of all, I had let Jim down.

The next morning, I resolved to tackle the situation. Working with our lawyer and accountant it took a few weeks to get everything lined up, but then I was ready. Eighteen months, one week and five days after Jim passed I sold the company to an American conglomerate with excellent environmental credentials. They bought Mighty Meat Pies in a contractual deal that saw the board replaced, pension plans and holiday benefit reinstated, and a bonus pay out to all staff who chose to stay. Mickey was re-appointed. Not as line manager, but as CEO of the brand. *I cut out the gristle for you, Jim.*

Tony was shocked, but he loved me and supported any decision I made. It took a few days for Isabelle to get her head round it all. On the Skype I explained I'd always be proud of Mighty Meat Pies, and everything her father had done in spearheading the international multi-million-pound brand, but that I needed the freedom to move on for me. I'd put the house in her name, so she would always have a base here if she wanted. Then I introduced her to Tony, and told her I was moving to LA. I knew she and the girls would love to come visit me, and Harry Potter's Hogsmeade at Universal Studios!

Two weeks before we were due to leave Tony came over in a terrible state. The buyer of his UK house had pulled out last minute, which meant he couldn't secure our new LA home, which meant he wouldn't qualify for his US visa, which he needed to work. And his work was his life. And because the purchase was abroad, the bank wouldn't provide a bridging loan. I said I would pay for the house. I had all this money sitting in my account and a million on a property in the U.S. felt like a good investment to me. You can't argue with bricks and mortar. But Tony explained the money had to come from him, in order for him to qualify for the visa. He was devastated that our plans were crumbling around us, when all he needed was a short-term loan from the bank.

I remember what it was like when Jim and I started out with just his dad's butcher's shop, which we inherited along with his father's debts. I remember trying to talk to the bank and it being like bashing my head against a brick wall. I said I'd transfer Tony the money. He refused. He tried a few more banks, hit more brick walls. Finally, for us, he relented and agreed to accept the money. But only as a loan until his house sold. And we were on our way again! That night we toasted our relationship with champagne. Our big adventure.

Perhaps it was in his eyes. The way he lifted his glass. The smile that played on his lips. But somewhere in that giddy bubbly night I knew. Something wasn't right.

Jim always said I had a good head on my shoulders. *You seem daft, girl, but god forbid anyone who underestimates you.* I know what I look like, what I sound like. I know my language can be a bit dated, and I call the internets by the wrong name. People see me as the silent smiling wife of Jim the local lad done good with his Mighty Meat Pie empire. What people don't know is it's my empire. Jim was all for cutting our losses when we inherited his dad's shop and debts. He thought he could get a job at the factory. It would have taken us years to pay it off. And I didn't want that. I was pregnant when I went to visit the banks and they rejected us for a loan. Some weeks we could only pay Mickey and there was nothing left for us. But I knew we had to diversify. Quality was always Jim's strength. We had to make other quality products. I started with meat pies. I'd stay up all night, baking, and we'd sell them in the shop. They were very popular. And when a local string of stores asked if we could give them 500 a day, I had Jim say yes even though we didn't know how we'd do it. In those days, round here, it didn't do to be a woman in business, so after the failed attempts at the bank, we always had Jim front every decision I took. He was a people person, always had been. But it was me who was the brains. Isabelle had been born and we were getting no sleep anyway, so we'd stay up baking to deliver the orders. And soon word spread about our quality pies. We got orders from restaurants, other shops. I took on one of the other mums to help cook. Then we got a small industrial kitchen. When the supermarket chain Booths placed an order, it was a turning point. I had Jim pitch Sainsbury's. And when that worked, I began to look further afield.

We invested in a trade fair table in America, taking an excited six-year-old Isabelle with us. Jim thought it would be a waste of money. And it was, for a week. But who should walk in with Mr Reagan and a news crew on the last day? Only Maggie Thatcher. She was doing her prime ministerial duties building trade between the nations. Jim and I have always voted Labour, but I whispered in Isabelle's ear to offer them some pie – and she did. They came over and Jim switched on the charm, played the son of a shopkeeper card. There was a moment when Mr Reagan got very confused when we mentioned jelly, which apparently means jam in American, and the cameras got it all. Next day that clip was on every American news channel, and orders for our pies came rolling in. We were a good team, Jim and I.

And now I could hear him in my head. *Always trust your instincts, girl, they've never let you down before.* I went to the gym I know Belinda Sharpe uses, and made sure I was outside when her yoga came out. After a small amount of chit chat I casually said I'd bumped into her friend Tony Waites. She didn't know who I was talking about. Turns out the silly woman has her privacy settings open on her Facebook. Anyone can see and comment on her posts. Next I called up Candice Duvall with a donation for her hospice, and asked if she could remember who it was she'd introduced me to on the Operatic Society's night. She could: a fantastic facialist called Brian! Could dear Milly Macclesfield let me have a copy of the invite list for her Cambodian fundraiser, as she'd done such a good job? No Tony anywhere on the list. He hadn't been unable to make it at the last minute, he'd never been invited in the first place. I realised with dawning horror I'd never been to his house. He always collected me from mine, which had seemed gentlemanly at the time. And we always stayed at mine because of the cats. Online I took a closer look at his Facebook account. Over three hundred friends. And every single one of them was a woman.

I was too embarrassed to talk to my own lawyer, so I found a man two hours away, what they call a private investigator, and paid him in cash. Within forty-eight hours he had amassed a horrible amount on Tony. Except that's not his real name. Tony, my Tony, is really called Richard. Richard Anthony Watson is unemployed and currently lives in a rented one bed flat (under his false name). He has moved frequently, uses multiple aliases, and has left behind him a string of broken hearted women he has defrauded. He doesn't even own a piano!

I felt sick reading the pain he had caused. And that he kept getting away with. Because if the women he cheated *were* brave enough to go to the police there was nothing they could do. They had willingly given him their money. He said it was a gift and there was never paperwork to prove otherwise. Tony, Richard, whoever he was, would simply change his name and resurface somewhere else with a new target in his sights. Previously the amounts had run to tens of thousands of pounds. He must have thought he'd hit the jackpot when I sold the company and suddenly had millions at my disposal. And I'd already transferred the money to him.

Tony's phone went straight to a message saying the number was unavailable. I'd been so foolish. No, I'd been broken by the loss of Jim, and Tony had taken advantage of that. But perhaps I could catch him before he went to ground. I jumped in the car and drove straight to the flat the private eye listed as "Tony Waite's" address. He was packing up when I arrived. He was shocked to see me. Tried to pretend everything was normal. But when I confronted him, when I started listing the names of all the other women he'd hurt, he actually had the audacity to laugh.

'*What are you going to do? Tell your girlfriends I only fucked you for the money? You women are all the same – stupid, vain sluts.*'

It was the first time I'd heard him use an obscenity. I think I was holding out hope until then that the situation could be fixed. But those words. His sneer. The way he roughly grabbed my arm to throw me out like rubbish. I was back in the bank, pregnant, begging for money and they were telling me they'd rather talk to my husband. I was watching Jim deliver the business proposals I'd written. I was being patronised by the board.

And I'd had enough of silently smiling.

SO, I'M FINALLY getting on that plane to see Isabelle. It's funny what you can learn on the internets. Like the UK has no extradition treaty with Japan. I found all the other women from the private investigator's list. They each received an unmarked envelope of cash through their door refunding what they lost. And 'Tony Waites' has gone. I've washed my hands of him. After I used Jim's old meat grinder. The cats ate the lot. It was self-defence, I struggled and he hit me. Not that it matters. There is no body, and who will miss a man who never existed in the first place?

Brick

Rachel Rivett

I HAD ALWAYS been afraid of life. It was why I didn't get involved. The girls at school called me Mouse, and they were right. I was a good sort, a brick: kind but timid. Unremarkable. The other Mistresses held hushed, brave, intelligent conversations but I pretended not to see. Averted my eyes.

Hands press down hard on my shoulders, ribs, breasts, in a brutal parody of intimacy. Hot tears sting my eyes and I squeeze them shut. Unbearable that this should be the first time I am touched. Violated by the very authorities I had always thought were there to protect me. The betrayal is absolute.

The suffragettes wore white, green and purple for purity of purpose, hope and integrity. I wore black. To mourn Emily and my own lack of courage. For my shame, so dark I thought I might implode with it.

The tube is filthy, caked with grime from previous abuses. Stained with blood. My stomach heaves.

I walked through the streets in a daze. Emily had died beneath the hooves of the King's horse. Proof of her emotional instability, they said. How dare they? Women in prison had died at the hands of the authorities, force fed into their lungs. And still nothing changed. Still no one cared. They painted pictures of the women as ugly old hags, militant and masculine, as if that in itself made a woman ridiculous. As if their lies were proof of our unworthiness. And people believed it. I even knew women who believed it.

Hard fingers prise my mouth open. The tube stabs into my throat and I gag.

But then a sound filled the streets. The ground thrummed with it. I felt it in the soles of my feet. An airship! Around me, the screaming started. People ran for cover. Had the enemy come? Had the Germans made it to London?

I stood still amongst the chaos, looking up. A woman stood in the airship basket; a man clambered, precarious, along the strut.

Votes for Women

The words shouted out, emblazoned on the side. I laughed, pure and strong for the first time in months. The beautiful, glorious audacity of it. Men and women together, fighting for justice. Leaflets fluttered down like flocks of doves: wild, free, ungovernable.

I am screaming but the only sound is a choking, gagging

bark, then even that stops. Pain sears me in places that will never heal. I stare into the dark of my closed eyes and see the leaflets raining down.

So, I take a brick. I can still feel the rough, gritty weight of it. The latent power. I take it and hurl it through the window of a shop. I imagine I am shattering the lies they are telling about us. Us.

I smile as I do it.

Because I know now that whether I am part of the fight or afraid to fight, the wrongness is not mine. The wrongness is in a system that denies us a voice.

I open my eyes. I hold the gaze of the woman who holds me down. My eyes blaze with the words I cannot say and startled, she steps back.

Know this. It is not over. We will fight for the vote. Then we will fight to change the system that does not think us, or anyone else, equal. We will not be governed by anyone who falsely believes themself superior. Until that day, when no one is held superior to another, we will fight.

We grow into our power. Our daughters will be stronger, and our daughters' daughters stronger still.

Until that day when government and justice are synonymous, know this: we will be wild, free, ungovernable. Not afraid to live.

AUTHOR BIOGRAPHIES

Isabel Costello
Isabel Costello is a London-based author and host of the Literary Sofa blog. Her debut novel *Paris Mon Amour* was published in 2016 and her short fiction has appeared in various magazines and anthologies. She teaches Resilient Thinking for Writers with psychologist and author Voula Tsoflias. @isabelcostello www.literarysofa.com

Christine Powell
Christine Powell lives in County Durham and is a member of Vane Women, a writers' co-operative dedicated to the promotion of the work of women writers in the north east of England (www.vanewomen.co.uk). Her stories have appeared in a number of anthologies and magazines.

Victoria Richards
Victoria Richards is a journalist and writer. In 2017/18 she was highly commended in the Bridport Prize, came third in *The London Magazine* short story competition and second in the TSS international flash fiction competition. She was also shortlisted in the Bath Novel

Award and the Lucy Cavendish Fiction Prize, and long listed in the National Poetry Competition. Find her at www.twitter.com/nakedvix and www.victoriarichards.co.uk.

Carolyn Sanderson

Carolyn Sanderson has worked in a number of fields, including teaching, training, counselling and working for the Church of England. She has written articles, reviews and a number of hymns. *Times and Seasons,* her contribution to the *Hometown Tales* series was recently published by Weidenfeld and Nicolson.

Sallie Anderson

Sallie Anderson is a writer living in Gloucestershire. She now works as a bookseller, but has had many jobs, including election polling clerk, which provided the inspiration for this story. Her short stories have been published in magazines and short-listed in a number of competitions. @JustSalGal

Abigail Rowe

Abigail Rowe lives and writes in Cork, Ireland. Currently completing her first novel, she delights in honing her craft writing short fiction, flash and the odd poem. Abigail's passions include bees, decent coffee, history, her grand-daughters and looking for beauty everywhere and anywhere she goes. twitter.com/RoweWrites and ismidlifeliminal.wordpress.com

Rosaleen Lynch

Rosaleen Lynch is an Irish community worker and writer in the East End of London. She pursues stories whether conversational, literary or performed, keen to explore them as part of the learning cycle of everyday life. @quotes_52 and www.52quotes.blogspot.com

Sophie Duffy

Sophie Duffy is the author of *The Generation Game*, *This Holey Life*, and *Bright Stars*. She has won the Yeovil Literary Prize, the Luke Bitmead Bursary, was runner-up for the Harry Bowling Prize and longlisted for the Guardian Not the Booker. She also writes as Lizzie Lovell and is part of the team of CreativeWritingMatters who administer the Exeter Novel Prize. She lives in Devon.

Kate Vine

Kate Vine is a graduate of the MA Creative Writing at the University of East Anglia. Her short fiction has been published by Dear Damsels and she is a recent winner of the City Writes competition. She is currently working on her first novel. @Kate_ElizabethV. twitter.com/Kate_ElizabethV and deardamsels.com/2018/02/16/he-loves-that-story

David Cook

David Cook's stories have been published in the *National Flash Fiction Anthology*, *Stories For Homes 2* and a number of online journals. He lives in Bridgend, Wales, with his wife and daughter. You can find more of his work at www.davewritesfiction.wordpress.com and @davidcook100.

Helen Irene Young

Helen is the author of *The May Queen* (Crooked Cat Books) and a digital editor for a book publisher. She attended the Faber Academy six-month novel writing course. She splits her time between London and Colombia, when she can get there. Her next novel, set in 1940s Bogotá, is about a broken architect trying to build something new. @helenireneyoung and www.helenirene young.com

Katherine Blessan

Katherine Blessan is the author of *Lydia's Song: The Story of a Child Lost and a Woman Found* (Instant Apostle, 2014), a hope-filled story about sex-trafficking in Cambodia. As well as writing her second novel, Katherine is a screenwriter and short story writer. She lives in Sheffield with her Indian husband and two children where she works as an English tutor and examiner. www.katherineblessan.com and @kathblessan

Anna Orridge

Anna Orridge has a Masters in Creative Writing with Distinction from the University of East Anglia. Her short stories have appeared in Mslexia, Paper Cuts and the

Retreat West anthology *Nothing Is As It Was*. She is currently writing a Middle Grade Fantasy novel in collaboration with Kickback Media.

Julie Bull

Julie Bull lives in South London and Sussex, where she also studied English Literature many moons ago. She is a recovering civil servant and now writes full time. Her first novel lives under the bed. Her short fiction has previously appeared in MIRonline. @juliebu72 instagram: juliebu72 Facebook: Julie Bull.

Karen Hamilton

Karen Hamilton caught the travel bug after a childhood spent abroad and worked as cabin crew for many years. *The Perfect Girlfriend* is her first novel. It is a psychological thriller about a sociopathic flight attendant, Juliette, who will stop at nothing to win back her pilot ex-boyfriend. @KJHAuthor

Angela Readman

Angela Readman's stories have won The Costa Short Story Award, The Mslexia Story Competition and been on Radio 4. Her debut collection *Don't Try This at Home (And Other Stories)* won The Rubery Book Award and was shortlisted in The Edge Hill Prize. She also writes poetry and is published by Nine Arches.

Anna Mazzola

Anna Mazzola is an award-winning writer of historical crime fiction. She has published two novels (*The Unseeing* and *The Story Keeper*) and several short stories. She is also a human rights solicitor. She lives in South London with two children, two cats and one husband. @Anna_Mazz and www.Annamazzola.com

Anne Hamilton

Anne Hamilton is a writer, tutor and editor of fiction, and the editor of online magazine, *Lothian Life*. Her stories are published in several journals and anthologies, and she has read at the Edinburgh International Book Festival. Her travelogue *A Blonde Bengali Wife*, inspired the charity, Bhola's Children, and she is now working on her second novel. Anne lives in Edinburgh, with her young son. www.writerightediting.co.uk and @Anne Hamilton7

Dane Divine

Dane Divine is an emerging writer from Plymouth, UK, where she completed her MA in Creative Writing. She now lives in Wellington, New Zealand where she works at an art college. Dane creates short stories and flash fiction. She is also working on a novel. instagram.com/ dane_divine

Cath Bore

Cath Bore is based in Liverpool. Her fiction and essays are published in Mslexia Magazine, Know Your Place: Essays on the Working Class (Dead Ink), National Flash Fiction Day Anthologies, I Hope You Like Feminist Rants, Fictive Dreams, Spontaneity and more. She also writes about music, books and pop culture. @cathbore and cathbore.wordpress.com

Taria Karillion

As the daughter of an antiquarian book dealer, Taria grew up surrounded by far more books than is healthy for one person. A literature degree, a journalism course and some gratuitous vocabulary overuse later, her stories have appeared in a Hagrid-sized handful of anthologies, and have won enough literary prizes to half-fill his other hand. Despite this, she has no need as yet for larger millinery.

Emily Kerr

Emily Kerr is proud to be a feminist. Her day job is as a journalist for ITV News and she spends her spare time writing fiction. Her novel *Who Does He Think He Is?* was shortlisted for the Joan Hessayon Award 2017. She is currently working on her second book. Twitter: @EmilyKerrWrites and www.emilykerrwrites.com

Angela Clarke

Angela Clarke is the award-winning, Sunday Times

bestselling author of the Social Media Murders, including *Follow Me, Watch Me,* and *Trust Me.* Her new novel is a gripping psychological thriller that highlights the plight of pregnant women in UK prisons: *On My Life* is out March 2019. www.AngelaClarke.co.uk

Rachel Rivett

Author of three picture books, *Little Grey and the Great Mystery, Are You Sad, Little Bear?* and *I Imagine*, Rachel Rivett has an MA in Writing for Children. She is happy to have short stories in anthologies with Mother's Milk and Retreat West. www.writewild.weebly.com

EDITOR BIOGRAPHIES

Amanda Saint

Amanda Saint founded and runs Retreat West, providing creative writing competitions and courses, and in 2017 launched Retreat West Books indie press. Her debut novel, *As If I Were A River*, was a NetGalley Top 10 Book of the Month and a Book Magnet Blog Top 20 Book of 2016. Her new novel, *Remember Tomorrow*, is coming in 2019. Her short stories have been widely published and been long and shortlisted for, and won, various prizes.

Rose McGinty

Rose McGinty is the author of *Electric Souk*. She lives in Kent and is a creative writing tutor and editor at Retreat West. Previously she worked for the NHS. Rose has won a number of writing competitions and had short stories selected for anthologies. She also enjoys running creative writing workshops in support of social causes. @rosemcginty

If you've enjoyed these stories, you can read more from some of the writers featured here, plus many other talented authors, in other Retreat West Books.

WHAT WAS LEFT, VARIOUS

20 winning and shortlisted stories from the 2016 Retreat West Short Story and Flash Fiction Prizes. A past that comes back to haunt a woman when she feels she has no future. A man with no mind of his own living a life of clichés. A teenage girl band that maybe never was. A dying millionaire's bizarre tasks for the family hoping to get his money. A granddaughter losing the grandfather she loves. A list of things about Abraham Lincoln that reveal both sadness and ambition for a modern day schoolgirl.

AS IF I WERE A RIVER, AMANDA SAINT

Kate's life is falling apart. Her husband has vanished without a trace – just like her mother did. Laura's about to do something that will change her family's lives forever – but she can't stop herself. Una's been keeping secrets – but for how much longer?

NOTHING IS AS IT WAS, VARIOUS

A charity anthology of climate-fiction stories raising funds for the Earth Day Network. A schoolboy inspired by a conservation hero to do his bit; a mother trying to save her family and her farm from drought; a world that doesn't get dark anymore; and a city that lives in a tower slowly being taken over by the sea.

SEPARATED FROM THE SEA, AMANDA HUGGINS

Separated From the Sea is the debut short story collection from award-winning author, Amanda Huggins. Crossing oceans from Japan to New York and from England to Havana, these stories are filled with a sense of yearning, of loss, of not quite belonging, of not being sure that things are what you thought they were. They are stories imbued with pathos and irony, humour and hope.

IMPERMANENT FACTS, VARIOUS

These 20 stories are the winners in the 2017 Retreat West Short Story and Flash Fiction prizes. A woman ventures out into a marsh at night seeking answers about herself that she cannot find; a man enjoys the solitude when his wife goes away for a few days; two young women make a get rich quick plan; and a father longs for the daughter that has gone to teach English in Japan.

http://retreatwestbooks.com

Lightning Source UK Ltd.
Milton Keynes UK
UKHW02f1147110918
328697UK00003B/21/P